Broken Sky

(#3)

Broken Sky

#3

Chris Wooding

Cover and illustrations by Steve Kyte

AN
APPLE
PAPERBACK

SCHOLASTIC INC.
New York Toronto London Auckland Sydney
Mexico City New Delhi Hong Kong

No part of this publication may be reproduced in whole or in part, or stored in a retrieval system or transmitted in any form or by any means, electronic, mechanical, photocopying, recording, or otherwise, without written permission of the publisher. For information regarding permission, write to Scholastic Ltd., Commonwealth House, 1-19 New Oxford Street, London WC1A 1NU, United Kingdom.

ISBN 0-439-12865-X

Text copyright © 1999 by Chris Wooding.

Illustrations copyright © 1999 by Steve Kyte.

All rights reserved. Published by Scholastic Inc., 555 Broadway, New York, NY 10012, by arrangement with Scholastic Ltd.

SCHOLASTIC and associated logos are trademarks and/or registered trademarks of Scholastic Inc.

12 11 10 9 8 7 6 5 4 3 2 1   0 1 2 3 4 5/0

Printed in the U.S.A.   40
First Scholastic printing, September 2000

Broken Sky

Act One
Part Seven

1

The Last and Only Piece

"Stay where you are," Tochaa ordered, his knives in his hands as the stranger hopped from his perch and dropped lithely to the ground.

Standing before them, on the crest of a shallow slope that fell away from the broken remains of a building, was an odd figure. He was of the Dominion-folk, perhaps the same age as Ryushi and Kia, and dressed in a ragged pair of trousers, battered boots, and little else except a set of wooden beads around his neck. His narrow face and lean body were covered in intricate skin-dye designs, and his hair clumped out in multicolored tufts from his scalp. On one hand was a thick black glove of leather and metal, and around his belt were more of his sharp throwing discs.

He obediently complied with Tochaa's order, leaning back against the wall and crossing his arms across his bare, thin chest; but his dog growled at the Kirin's tone from where it stood over the corpse of a Snapper.

"Call your dog."

"Anyone hurt?" the stranger asked.

"Call your dog," Tochaa repeated firmly.

The boy paused for a moment, then shrugged. "Come on, Blink," he said, not taking his eyes off Tochaa. The dog loped over to him and sat on its haunches by his side, protectively. Elani watched it nervously from behind Hochi. It was big, *really* big, with a short grey coat and taut muscles beneath.

"Who are you?" Tochaa demanded, his voice calm, his knives still held at the ready.

"You're too cautious," the boy replied casually. "If I wanted to hurt you, I'd have just left those Snappers to do the job for me."

"That's not an answer," Tochaa said.

"Are you Kirins all this pleasant? Who are *you*, that's what I wanna know. I'm curious as to whether or not it was worth my while helping you out."

"Tochaa, he *did* pretty much pull us out of the fire," Gerdi pointed out.

"Look, there's five of you and just two of us," the stranger said. "I just wanna talk with you."

"There are *six* of us," Elani muttered sulkily under her breath.

"So talk," Tochaa said.

"Y'know, weapons imply mistrust," came the reply, "and that kinda gets us off on the wrong foot."

Tochaa paused for a time, considering. He was weighing up the dangers of trusting this boy against the advantages that he might be able to give them if they engaged him in conversation; and he plainly wasn't going to talk to them while he was still being threatened.

"Anyone hurt?" the stranger asked again. "Your friend looked like he took a pretty nasty hit."

Hochi raised a hand to stay his concern. "I'm fine," he said. "Close call, that's all."

Tochaa, in the meantime, appeared to come to a decision. He sheathed his knives. "Okay," he said to the stranger. "We can talk."

"Good," the boy replied, walking over to them. His dog matched his pace, accompanying him. "I'm Whist, and this is Blink. You're new here, huh?"

"Just arrived," Tochaa said, still wary.

"Yeah, I can tell. No tribal colors, for one thing." Whist sauntered among them casually, retrieving his disc from the corpse of the Snapper with his armoured glove. He gave Elani a friendly smile, and she smiled back at him, surprised, then ducked away when Blink came to sniff at her.

"Are *you* from a tribe?" Ryushi asked.

"Me? Nah. Not my style. Just me and Blink, these last few years."

"Years?" Gerdi said.

Whist caught himself and gave a short laugh. "Years. Guess old habits die hard. There's no time in this place. No seasons, no days, not even any Glimmer plants to tell the time by," he said, giving the younger boy a somber glance. "You'll spend the rest of your life here. You'll get to know that." He wandered off a little way to rifle through the pockets of some of the dead that were scattered around, dark shapes in the twilight. "Not that there'll be much of it. Most new folk end up like these guys before too long."

"*You've* survived, though," said Hochi. "And on your own."

Blink whined, as if offended at being forgotten. Whist squatted next to the huge dog and patted him. "We know how to. Getting with the tribes might seem like a good idea, but you never know who's gonna win the next war. Nothing stays safe forever, not in this place. My way, I only have myself and my dog to worry about. It's easier to stay out of the way with just the two of us."

Tochaa looked at him, suspicion still mirrored in his cream-irised eyes. "Why *did* you help us out?"

"I hate Snappers," Whist said, shrugging his bare shoulders. "The less of 'em, the better. And I was curious. Good deed, if you like. Wouldn't want to see you get killed on your first day here." He looked up at the dark sun above them. "Huh! Did it again. Your first *day*? As if there's day or night in this place." He glanced at Tochaa. "But I suppose you're used to that."

"Do you know someone called Ty?" Kia asked suddenly. "Have you heard the name?"

Whist paused for a moment, considering. "No," he said at length. "Never heard it. Wait, you actually *know* someone in this place?"

"We came looking for him," Kia said.

"Does that mean you've got a way *out*?" Whist asked, suddenly interested, his painted face animated. "I mean, you couldn't possibly be stupid enough to come into Os Dakar of your own free will, if you couldn't get out again!"

Tochaa glared at Kia, warning her not to say any

5

more. She ignored him. "We need to find my friend," she said. "If you can take us to him, we can get you out."

"Kia!" Hochi exclaimed.

"How? How are you gonna escape?" Whist asked. There was an edge of feverish hope to his voice now.

"You'll know when the time comes," said Kia. "If you can keep your end of the bargain."

"*Can* I! I'll do anything you *want*!" Whist cried, then suddenly sobered. "But if you're lying about this, just re-member . . . I'm not a good person to have as an enemy."

"I'm not lying. Do we have a deal?" Kia said.

"Deal," he agreed. He looked around at them, dark eyes bright beneath his multicolored hair. "But first things first; let's get out of sight. I got a place. Follow me."

Without waiting to see if they were coming, he turned and began to hurry excitedly away, Blink loping at his side.

"Do we go?" Hochi asked, looking around at the oth-ers.

"Do we have a choice?" Tochaa said, and began to follow.

*   *   *

Whist's home was not far, although the route was tortuous and difficult. He took them up a steep, rocky incline before leading them to the edge of a wide, circular shaft in the stone, a hundred feet or more in diameter. Beneath, a long way down, was a sheltered clearing, where a murky pool lay at the bottom. The faint sun filtered down a meager glow into the sheer-sided pit, the stars dim sparks in the water.

Whist led them confidently to a near-invisible crevice near the top of the shaft, hidden by straggling bushes and rocks. It opened into a tight climb downward, a narrow split in the stone that allowed them to make a clambering descent through the darkness, before disgorging them at the foot of the pit. There they found themselves on the shore of the pool, looking at a scrappy assembly of logs of wood, moss, and skins, standing on thick stilts in the water. A narrow jetty led to the door.

Whist led them inside, chattering incessantly about how there were lots of things that lived in the ground that meant it was safer to be out on the water; how he'd found it one day, already built by some previous prisoners of Os Dakar who were now long gone; and how this place was his secret, and nobody else knew of it. Kia found that faintly hard to believe, if only because he was such a strangely open and honest character. At the

7

prospect of their deal, he had become almost painfully trusting of them, and acted as if they had known one another all their lives. Even the slightest glimmer of a chance at escape had ensured his complete loyalty. This was a strange place, she decided, and strange places breed strange characters. Or desperate ones.

Inside the house it was very cramped, as it had only been built for two, but they managed to find space. There was little furniture, only a small stool made out of a chopped log and a flat stone over which a cooking-pot hung, and in which the ashes of a fire lay blackened. More of a shelter than a home, really.

Whist apologized for having no firewood, saying that the reason he happened upon them today was because he had gone out to collect some, and he had gotten side-tracked. Instead of hot food, he offered them bowls of a hard, nutty cereal, which he told them he had stolen from the plantations of one of the tribes. It was dry and bland, but they could not refuse, and offered him some of their own rations in return, which he gratefully accepted.

They ate in the light of a single glowstone, which Gerdi brought from his pack and unwrapped to fend off the constant twilight. Cramped together, they huddled in the orange gloom. When they had finished, Whist looked from one face to another and said, "So now what?"

"You can start by telling us what happened back at the stockade," Tochaa said, remembering the terrible destruction and debris.

Whist was sitting cross-legged on the floor next to his dog, who stood alert, guarding him. "Tribe wars. They're always fighting, for food and so on. Gives 'em something to do, I guess. It's been happening a lot recently. Those red and blue warriors . . . they're from the Fallen Sun tribe. The others are the . . . Forgotten Legion or something. I forget. Stupid names. Anyway," he said, waving away the matter, "the Fallen Suns have got 'emselves some kind of new weapon. A war machine. They call it the Bear Claw. And until someone comes up with some way to stop it, they're pretty much invincible right now. I've seen it in action." He shrugged. "I figure they're gonna milk their advantage as long as they can. Wipe out the other tribes. Gather power to 'emselves."

"A machine?" Ryushi asked.

"Well, more like a vehicle," Whist corrected himself.

"Like a cricktrack, right?" Elani put in.

"Much bigger," he said. Blink snuffed next to him and put his head on his paws, relaxing.

"But, how can that be?" Kia asked. "To make something like that, you'd need Metalsmiths, Machinists . . . a Pilot. . . ." Her voice trailed off.

9

"Metalsmiths and Machinists they got," Whist said, rubbing his skin-dyed cheek with his knuckles absently. "A Pilot to run the thing . . . well, that they don't got until recently."

"They've got a Pilot?" Kia asked urgently. Everybody else looked up at her. Blink's ears lifted in interest.

"Only one on Os Dakar, way I hear," Whist said. "Is that important?"

"It's Ty!" she said. "It has to be!"

"*That's* your friend? The *Pilot*? Why didn't you say?"

"You know where he is?" Kia asked, a spark of hope creeping on to her face as she spoke.

"Sure I do. Well, I mean, I know where the Fallen Sun stockade is, and if he's anywhere he's gonna be there."

"Can you take us?" she asked urgently.

"Can you get me out of here?" he countered.

"Yes!"

"Then yeah," said Whist, shrugging again. "No problem at all."

"Kia, Kia, wait a minute," Hochi put in. "Calm down. You have to think about what you're doing."

"I *know* what I'm doing," she snapped at him, a feverish glint in her eyes. "I'm going in there to get him."

"You think they're going to let him go that easily?" Tochaa asked, his infuriatingly reasonable voice cutting through Kia's mania. "He's the only Pilot they've got, re-member. Who'll power the Bear Claw without him?" His light gaze met hers. "They'll not give up their great-est advantage."

"So what do you propose? That we do *nothing*? I'll go myself if I have to!" Kia declared angrily, her face twist-ing in the shadows of the glowstone.

"Not without me," Ryushi said, shifting forward in the huddle of bodies. "I'm coming, too."

"We'll all go," Whist said. "We just have to —"

"We *won't* all go," put in Tochaa, quieting everyone. "We won't. We can't just break in there and get him out. We'll achieve nothing by force. Two of us — *just* two, any more and we'll be spotted for sure — will sneak in there with Whist and bring Ty out with them. The rest of us stay here."

"Just two of you?" Whist queried. "But that's —"

"Whatever it is, it's better than seven of us blundering around and getting caught. The smaller the number who go, the better. And if they get captured, there's some of us left behind to get them out."

Whist was silent. He seemed a little unhappy about Tochaa's decision, but he didn't try to change his mind.

"But how will we know if they're caught?" Elani piped up.

"We'll give them twelve hours. If they're not back by then, we go and get them."

"How are you gonna count the hours, bright spark?" Whist asked.

"We're wasting time," Kia said quickly, before an argument could arise. "Two of us. That's me and Gerdi." She turned to her brother, who looked shocked and hurt in the orange light, and said: "He's better at it than you are. It's tactical sense."

"Hey, wait, this isn't all decided yet," Hochi said. "Now why don't we —"

"It *is* decided, Hochi," Kia said firmly, the words falling out of her in a jumble. "It's decided because he's *my* friend and he nearly sacrificed himself for us back at the Stud and he's the last and only piece left of my life before I got tangled up in all of *this*!" She paused, daring anyone to challenge her. "Nobody's leader here. I made a deal with Whist. He's gonna keep his end of the bargain, and then I'm gonna keep mine. Gerdi, are you with me?"

"Course I am," he said, grinning. "It'll be easy as stealing pastries from a fat man."

Hochi's face colored in anger, but the younger boy was too far away to reach, and the room was too cramped.

12

"Then it's settled," Kia said. "We go as soon as we can."

Ryushi was silent. Here was the sister he had come to know. Hard, commanding, strong. She was driven, pushed on by a force that he could not wholly *identify*, towards a goal that he was not sure existed. Perhaps saving Ty was the only way she could regain what had been lost at Osaka Stud. That was what *she* thought, at least. Occasionally, he caught glimpses of the old Kia pushing through; but mostly, she existed behind a shield of cold efficiency, unwilling to let feelings or desires get in her way.

Maybe finding Ty could change all that. Ryushi didn't know.

He just wanted his sister back.

2

Hope This Key

Inside the heavily fortified stockade of the Fallen Sun tribe, on the prison plateau of Os Dakar, there was an intruder. He slipped between the bright pools of light thrown by the torches in their sconces, sheltering in the safety of the permanent twilight of Kirin Taq. A faint bubble of rough laughter, far away, reached his ears. The camp smelled of smoked meat and sweat, and a hundred different man-scents. But there was no time to investigate the multitude of exciting sensations that surrounded him. For now, Blink the dog had a task to complete.

He padded through the camp, a lean, loping grey shape, his head hanging low between his high shoulders. His canine mind paid no attention to the close-built buildings, ramshackle constructions cobbled together

14

with whatever resources were at hand. It had no interest in the curious, haphazard way that wood meshed with thatch, stone with plates of metal, a jumbled nightmare of unskilled architecture, built out of necessity by desperate people in a desperate place.

But the presence that rode behind his eyes noted it all.

The approaching sound of footsteps on the gravelly ground reached Blink's ears, but the smell of liquor-sweat on the breeze had alerted him a long few seconds earlier, and he had slipped smoothly out of sight, lying down in the shadow of a woodpile covered by tarp. Two man-voices, getting louder as they neared. He did not know what they were doing, only that Whist-master didn't want him to be spotted, and that he had to hide. The words meant nothing to him, only the tone of voice in which they were spoken. Companionable. Relaxed.

He listened anyway. Something inside compelled him to. And though the words to him were a mush of incoherent sounds, a small part of him-that-was-not-him understood every word.

". . . about Semper. Still, he got 'im venged. Just as he was falling, Semper took 'im slidewise on the cheek with 'is hooking-flail, nai? He brung his enemy down withly."

"Old Semper. Never was one to go down quietsome, nai?"

"A toasting," declared the first voice. "To battle, and to a battle fought quicklean and victorious."

"And to the stripling Ty, and the crushcrumping Bear Claw."

A clinking of metal mugs, and their drinking carried them away as their footsteps faded. The name they spoke was somehow familiar to Blink, but he was unable to attach any sensations to it, whether good or bad. The presence riding with him was interested by the sound, however, so he decided *Ty* meant a good thing, and thumped his tail quietly on the ground.

Once the men had passed, and no other danger-scents were nearby, Blink loped out of the deeper shadows and headed further into the camp. There was an image of something in his mind, something that he needed to get, to fetch for his master. Strange, really, because it was something that would ordinarily hold no interest for him at all. It was not food, it didn't smell of anything much, and it would provide him no amusement. But Whist-master wanted it, and he wanted Blink to get it. He would do it because it would make Whist-master happy, and that made *him* happy. His tail wagging again at the thought, he slipped around the edge of a bright smudge of torchlight and padded between two close-leaning buildings, disappearing into the blackness.

He knew where he was going. He'd been here before, many times. There were very few places in Os Dakar where Blink hadn't been. It was his territory. Once, he had lived outside, in another time, in a sun-bright place where his skin was hot and gnats and midges wheeled in the air during summertime, and then the world would turn white and he would frolic and snuff in the cold-white-crisp with Whist-master. Then the black-hard-skins had taken him, him and Whist-master to this place, and they had put Whist-master in the slide-to-water, and they were going to keep him but he broke free and followed Whist-master. Now Os Dakar was his territory. No dogs, only Snappers and humans and worse things. But at least he had Whist-master.

For now, though, he had a purpose. An object, to fetch for Whist-master. And from somewhere deep inside him, he knew where it would be. Not knew as a dog knew — dogs *knew* something because it *was* — but as a human knew, as an assumption: that the place where he was going was the most likely place to find what he was looking for. That knowledge came from the presence who rode with him, sharing his thoughts.

So he came to the building that matched the one in

his mind. It stood alone, three stories high, a lower floor of stone and two upper floors of planks and logs. A balcony ran around its waist, an uneven wooden handrail following it. At each corner of the balcony, a man stood, watching the short approach to the building. All of the men here were painted, half blue and half red, with their heads hairless. Blink couldn't see in color, only different shades of gray, but the presence in his mind filled in the detail. Those men were in the way of what he had to get.

He snorted, pawing behind his ear to scratch an itchy spot there. He didn't want to be seen; Whist-master wouldn't want that, and it would be bad for him. He didn't think the two-color men meant him harm, but they would see him if he tried to get closer to the building.

He padded out into the light, foreleg raised in a step. He blinked.

And the pad of his foot landed on wooden boards. He looked around and listened. Nobody was inside. No torch burned to illuminate the interior, which was strewn with interesting relics, bits of junk and semi-eaten food. The man-scent here was strong, but it was hours old. The only men were out on the balcony, and though he couldn't see them through the small wind-holes, he knew they were there.

The presence behind his eyes was urging him to hurry, but his curiosity got the better of him for a moment, and he could not resist nosing around all the strange articles that lay about the floor or on rickety shelves. He scarfed up a cold Snapper-leg with only one bite taken out of it, gnawing at the tough meat, but caution urged him not to crunch the bones, fearful of the noise it would make. After a few moments, his small rebellion satisfied, he found stairs and climbed them warily.

At the top was another room, this one heavy with night-sweat and sleep-smell. There was a bed here, a wooden pallet covered with many coarse blankets. He sniffed it over.

That is Kettin-leader-smell, he thought, finding the file in his mental library. He had smelled it before, and often.

Returning to the task at hand, he looked around for what he had been sent to fetch. The slight tang of metal-scent told him where it was a moment before his eyes did. A heavy key, hanging on a hook above the bed. Padding over to it, Blink stood up to his full height, leaning his forepaws on the wall. He was a huge dog, and as tall as a man in that position. Carefully, he bent his head and fastened his teeth around the handle of the key,

19

then shook it off the hook. It dropped to the floor with a clang. The presence in his mind flashed a warning, but he unconcernedly dropped back to all fours and gathered it up in his mouth. *Whist-master would be happy with him,* he thought, as his tail began to wag.

He blinked, and a moment later the room was empty, with only the missing key to show that the dog had ever been there at all.

"He's on his way back," Whist said.

Gerdi shifted his weight uncomfortably. They were lying under the sparse cover of a fringe of gnarled bushes that lined the edge of a stony trench, a stream that had long since dried up. It had been hard enough to get themselves there undetected, with the amount of patrols that they had encountered on the way. Now that they were there, they dared not leave their shelter, and they had become stiff and sore from lying among the thin, tough bushes.

"This place has better security than anywhere in Tusami City I could name," Gerdi muttered bitterly, as another pair of watchful eyes passed close to where they lay.

"This place needs it," Whist replied simply.

A little further on from where they were, the streambed abruptly ended in a haphazard scramble of rocks and boulders. To unsuspecting eyes, it looked like the water had long ago undermined a section of the ground and it had collapsed, damming the flow and strangling the river. But Whist said different.

"Y'know, every fortress has got a bolt-hole," he told them. "The first rule of survival is not to let yourself get trapped. Kettin, the head guy of the Fallen Sun, he's smart. He knows that. Hidden behind that rockfall is a secret tunnel that leads to the stockade."

"Not secret enough so you don't know about it," Kia observed, from where she was lying next to him.

Whist smiled quirkily, the skin-dye designs on his face curling with his lip. "Nothing on Os Dakar is secret enough so I don't know about it," he said, then returned his gaze to the streambed. "Me and Blink, anyway."

"You ever used it before?" Gerdi asked.

"Never needed to," came the reply. "I figure a man's secret exit is his own business." He grinned. "At least until I stand to gain something from it. We *are* getting off this place, right?"

"Every exit is an entrance," said Kia philosophically, ignoring his question, which was more for reassurance than anything else.

Whist looked at her oddly. "Course it is," he said. "But anyhow, I can get the key, but once we're in there,

I dunno what we'll come across. Maybe guards, maybe nothing."

"I can handle it from there," said Gerdi. "I'm not *totally* useless, y'know. I'm good for more than just bugging Hochi."

"Here he is," said Whist, a moment before Blink suddenly appeared in the streambed in front of them, literally blipping into existence in the space of a fraction of a heartbeat. He loped up the bank and into the bushes where they waited, squashing himself low. Dangling from his mouth was a big, heavy iron key. He dropped it in front of Whist, then began to bustle excitedly around, nuzzling his master's face, treading on the others' hands, and generally making a nuisance of himself. Whist made a fuss of him, scratching him behind his ears and on his back, and he *whuffed* quietly with pleasure.

"How does he *do* that?" Gerdi asked. "I'd almost be jealous, if he didn't smell like a heap of dead horses."

"The blinking thing?" Whist replied absently. "I dunno. They can all do it, his kind. They live up near where I come from, in the Wildlands. We call them Flicker Dogs. You'd often see them out hunting, but always in the distance. Nobody ever got close to them. They'd just disappear."

"So what's the story with Blink?" Gerdi asked, shoving an errant paw out of his face with an expression of irritation.

"Oh, he found me," Whist said. "He came to me just after my eighth winter, and he's been with me ever since. He can leave when he wants."

"The stones?" Kia asked, glancing at the three small, silver ovals that studded Whist's spine, nestling among the swirls of skin-dye.

"Yeah," he said. "Me and Blink are kinda close. It's a gift." Leaving the explanation hanging, he scooped up the key and quieted the dog. "Anyway, let's go. This friend of yours better be worth it."

"He's your ticket out of here," Kia said, a slight harshness creeping into her tone. "Do *you* think he's worth it?"

"That depends," he replied. "On whether or not we get out of that stockade alive."

The patrols that they occasionally glimpsed were not like those of the Keriags, around the perimeter of the plateau. Instead of the rigid pattern of the insectile creatures, they were random and unevenly spaced. Kia thought it smacked of disorganization, but Whist assured her that that was only the impression it was sup-

23

posed to give. The Fallen Sun were a tight and rigidly disciplined unit. But as Whist seemed to have an uncanny ability to guess when the next patrol would turn up, they had to trust him to decide when to make their way out of cover and along the streambed.

"Now," he said.

They slid out from the bushes and into the trench, Blink following them down in a canine scramble of loose stones. Kia had cause to be thankful for the feeble sun of Kirin Taq as they hurried through the shadows, for it provided them enough illumination to see by while keeping them relatively invisible from above. They reached the rockfall without being seen, Blink taking the lead. Kia caught a flash of the gray body bounding ahead before it disappeared.

Kia hesitated for a moment. It almost seemed as if he had run into the rockslide and winked out of existence. But then he was back, appearing from behind a boulder, looking at them expectantly as if to say: *What are you waiting for?* She took a few steps closer, and was surprised to see that, behind a boulder that she had thought was rammed up hard against the wall, there was a narrow crack, big enough to squeeze through. In the twilight, it looked like just another shadow; if it weren't for the dog standing half in and out of it, she wouldn't have realized what it was.

"That's it?" she asked.

Whist smiled at Kia's expression. "Hard to see, isn't it?" he said. "Course, the bad light helps hide it. Blink found it a year or so ago. You can hide things from us humans easy, but a dog is a different matter."

Inside, the darkness was absolute. Gerdi brought out his glowstone, bundled in a rag. He was about to unwrap it when Whist stayed his hand.

"Don't. Not yet. They'll spot the light from outside. Just feel your way."

So they did, squeezing themselves through the narrow passageway, their hands and backs pressed up against the cold stone as they shuffled along. They could hear the scratch of Blink's nails on the ground, somewhere ahead, scouting out the route for them. He needn't have bothered; there was only one way to go, and that was onward.

"Here we are," Whist whispered after a short time, and the wall curved away from their hands, leaving them anchorless in the endless black. They had the impression of being in a small open space, but they could not have said how they knew that. Perhaps it was the change in sound of their quiet footsteps.

"From here on in, I don't know what we'll find," Whist advised them in a hushed voice. "Be ready. We may have to fight."

There was a shuffling in the darkness, then the sound of the heavy key sliding into the lock, and the turning of the tumblers, deep within the door.

"Ready?" Whist asked, flexing his thick glove and running his other hand over the flat sides of the throwing discs at his belt.

Kia tested the grip on her staff. Gerdi loaded his crossbow. "Ready," they replied.

Whist put his shoulder to the door and pushed inward.

The door opened into further darkness.

"Glowstone?" Gerdi suggested.

"Glowstone," Whist agreed. They were far enough inside the passage now so that their light would not be seen from outside.

Gerdi unwrapped his stone, and the soft orange glow swelled around them. They were in a bare stone corridor, with mold growing between the bricks. It was damp and smelled unhealthy, and it extended beyond the range of the glowstone's illumination, where there was only black.

"Let's go," Gerdi said.

They walked onward, following the corridor for a way before it ended in a set of steps, leading up to a trapdoor. By cloaking the glowstone, they could see that there was dim light on the other side. Whist pushed it softly. It came open, but only by six inches or so, before a chain stopped its progress. He pressed his head up against the gap, squashing his multicolored hair flat, and looked out.

They were surrounded by logs, smelling heavily of wood rot, piled all around the trapdoor. Whist craned his neck, trying to look around, but his limited field of view revealed nothing more. He tested the chain by pushing against the trapdoor, and heard a sliding of weighted metal above him. Reaching around, he felt the chunky shape of a metal padlock.

"Can we get through?" Kia asked quietly from below.

"Maybe," he said. "Let's hope this key fits both locks."

He reached his arm through the gap, right up to the shoulder, and twisted his wrist around as far as he could, the key in his grip. For a few moments, he fumbled around; then the barrel of the key found the keyhole, and he turned it sharply. The padlock fell away, and the chain rattled free. Long seconds passed while everyone held their breath, but it seemed that nobody had heard. Whist put his back to the trapdoor and pushed it open, and this time there was no resistance. They were in.

They found themselves in a high-ceilinged cave, in the midst of what appeared to be a disused corner of a huge wood storeroom. Clusters of logs, bundles of sticks, and sacks of wood shavings were hoarded here, piled higher than their heads; but they appeared to be in a little-visited section of the cave, for here much of the wood had rotted or was infested with mold or weevils. Blink snuffed around, investigating his new surroundings. Whist pointed to where a break in the piles of wood formed a narrow path, winding between the carefully stacked supplies.

"That way," he said quietly. "Let's go."

They secured the padlock again, so as not to arouse the suspicions of anyone who might come investigating, and then crept onward. Blink fell into step beside them. Kia glanced at him. It was as if the dog understood the need for stealth, and was purposely curbing its natural instincts to bark or run around and explore ahead. She looked at Whist, the strange boy with his lean, naked torso a colorful mess of designs, and at the three silver ovals on his back. What kind of bond did they share, really? Where did Blink stop and Whist begin?

They made their way along the aisles between the high stacks, forging through the faint light with Gerdi's glowstone stashed away again. The storage cave was not large, but Kia had to admit that Whist had been right about how organized the Fallen Sun tribe were. Here were woven hemp sacks to store the wood in, and carefully arranged logs for burning and building. It was the work of a community, not just a band of cutthroats as the obvious evidence would have them believe.

Without incident, they reached the mouth of the cave where the stacks of logs abruptly ended and the camp opened out in a crazed clutter of piecemeal buildings, accented by the flickering blaze of torches. Pressed back in the shadows, they could see the tribesmen of the Fallen Sun nearby, clustered around fires drinking rough wine or engaged with some work of their own. The light of the blazes showed off their tribal skin colors: blue on the left side of their bodies, and red on the right, with shaven heads. Mostly they wore furs, but the odd few had clothes of wool or higher quality fabric. They carried weighted bola on their belts: three linked chains with heavy iron balls on their ends, each one bearing a hooked blade. It seemed to be the tribal weapon.

"Come on," Whist said. "I've been in and out of here a hundred times. They don't think anything can get past their stockade. Just stay quiet, and it'll be easy."

He slunk out into the shadows, skirting the edge of the woodpiles. Blink went with him, surprisingly lithe and quiet considering his size. Kia and Gerdi followed, keeping their eyes on the men nearby, sheltering in the darkness.

They made their way around the edge of the camp by creeping from cover to cover, each time pausing to be sure the coast was clear before going on. It was slow, painstaking going, but Whist seemed to know what he was doing, and they were rarely in any danger of being seen. Eventually, he began to lead them further into the camp, where the buildings crowded up close together. Both the amount of cover and the amount of danger increased, and they found themselves breathlessly ducking away to avoid being seen as tribesmen appeared out of nowhere to cross their path. When Whist called a halt and announced that they had reached Ty's quarters, their relief was evident on their faces.

It was a low building, two squat stories piled on top of each other, with a section of one wall made of mud and clay while the rest was made of unevenly hewn stone. The upper story was smaller than the lower one, and the difference in size left a balcony ledge running around it, about four feet wide.

"He'll be on the second story," Whist advised. "We can get up there by climbing to the ledge."

The lumpy stone provided plenty of handholds, and the climb was short and easy, though Kia's staff had to be passed up to her by Gerdi. They chose the side where a nearby building would screen them from sight, and when they pulled themselves up, they found Blink waiting for them, having opted not to climb but to wink up to the ledge.

"When we walk around the other side, there's a door," Whist said. "Ty should be in there. Thing is, we'll be able to be seen from all around, so we gotta hurry."

Kia took a breath. "I'll go first," she said. "I want to see him."

Whist nodded gravely. "I'll go with you. Gerdi can stay with Blink."

Gerdi shrugged in agreement, and Kia nodded absently, peering around the corner at the short, exposed distance they would have to make, and the gravelly clearing below. A pair, a man and a woman, were walking across it, talking raucously. She waited for them to go, barely able to contain herself, and then she and Whist made their move.

They followed the ledge around to the other side of the building, where torches threw their shadows long across the stone. Kia had almost forgotten about the danger they were in by now. As she had gotten closer and closer to meeting Ty, she had become more and more focused on the thought of what she would say when she saw him, of how it would feel. Would the terrible numbness in her finally disappear? Would the aching void in the pit of her stomach be filled? Would it be, at least to some degree, like it was before the horrors began?

She hurried to the door, Whist close behind. She put her hand on the handle and turned it. It was as if she were working on automatic, no longer in control of herself, watching only as an observer. She pushed the door open.

Ty.

And at that moment, a thought struck her with sickening clarity.

How did Whist know where Ty's quarters were?

But it came too late. The door was already open. Inside, the six Fallen Sun tribesmen that had been sitting in their barracks were standing up as they saw her, their hands reaching for their weapons. Kia felt the cold press of steel against her throat, the pricking edge of a blade, and her heart sank.

"Surprise," Whist said in her ear.

3

The Buck of the Catch

Kia sat with her back against the hard rock, her head resting on her knees, hugging herself. She was in a tiny alcove, barely big enough to stand up in, hemmed in by rough, worn stone. In front of her, a foot or so beyond her toes, a heavy iron grille cast squares of bluish light across her huddled silhouette.

Outside, the mob of tribesmen were chanting, working themselves up into a frenzy of anticipation.

The Snapper Run was at hand.

Kia felt sick. All along, when Tochaa had repeatedly warned them what a dangerous place Os Dakar was, she had paid him scant attention. She had thought only of Ty. She had become so caught up in the idea of his rescue, she had blinded herself to everything else. And

Whist had duped them. He'd sold them into the hands of the Fallen Sun. Probably it was part of a deal he had going with them; he would deliver them any newcomers that arrived, in return for them leaving him and Blink alone. She didn't know. Perhaps she'd never know. On Os Dakar, in a world of desperate people fighting to survive, who could tell what passed for logic or honor?

She'd been naïve. Naïve and stupid. She'd thought that because she had promised to get Whist out with them she'd secured his absolute loyalty. Maybe in the outside world it would be true, but she doubted even that. Once again, she had been taught a painful lesson in the realities of the life outside her sheltered childhood. Perhaps Whist had thought she was lying when she said they had an escape plan. After all, what had she done to make him trust her any more than the next person on Os Dakar? Maybe he had thought that the safer option was to deliver them up to the most powerful tribe on the plateau. At least then he would have some tangible reward.

So many questions, and no answers. And no Ty.

They'd captured Gerdi easily. With Whist's knife at her throat, he'd had no choice but to surrender. Kia couldn't bring her stones into action fast enough to prevent her throat being cut, so she'd had little option, either. She'd decided to bide her time, waiting until she would have an opportunity to use her stones to escape or attack. They couldn't keep her imprisoned, not with the power she wielded.

That was when she discovered another previously unknown aspect of the real world. Damper Collars. Thin bands of strong metal, affixed around the neck, with a single ice-white stone at the throat. How they worked, she didn't know. All she knew was that once that collar was put around her, her stones were useless. No matter how hard she tried, she could not summon a reaction from them. No Flow. Nothing.

Stupid, *stupid*. Now that she had time to think back, she realized that Whist's talk had been full of contradictions. Hadn't he said he'd never used the tunnel, and then later boasted he'd been in and out of the stockade a hundred times? And how did he know where the key was kept, and where Ty would be? And how had he predicted the pattern of the patrols outside with such uncanny accuracy? He was plainly familiar with the place, but Kia had been too focused on her own concerns to see it.

And now she was here, in what the tribesmen called the Snapper Run. Gerdi was in a similar tiny cell, close by. She wondered what had happened to the others, back at Whist's home, and what it would have been like if Tochaa had not insisted that some of them stay behind. The Kirin had been right to be suspicious of Whist; and they should have heeded his warnings about how dangerous Os Dakar really was.

She raised her head from her knees and looked out through the bars of the grille. Out there was the arena. A vast, sheer-sided pit, pocked with small, barred alcoves similar to the one she was held in. Ledges, walkways, platforms, and pillars crisscrossed the pit from the bottom to near the top, all fashioned from stone, a multi-level maze of paths. The central point was a tall, hollow pillar, studded with fist-sized holes at even intervals up its length. At the top of this, hanging in a stone cradle, was a huge wooden vat, sloshing with gallons of foul, brackish water, in which were floating many wooden balls, each about the size of a kuja fruit. It was attached by a rope to an iron crank, out of reach on the lip of the pit.

Ringing the top of the pit were the spectators, cheering and jeering impatiently for the game to begin. Kia's gate was high up, near the top of the arena. She had not been told the rules, so she assumed that there were none. She had no idea how the game was played or what was going to happen. She knew only that they had left her and Gerdi's weapons in the middle of the arena floor, a fair way below them, and that she was heading for them the minute her gate opened.

She flexed her shoulders. The tension in the air was mounting. Somehow, she knew: The Snapper Run was about to begin.

A tribesman began to work the crank, pumping it back and forth. The crowd erupted in a boisterous cheer. The rope tightened. The vat of water began to tip, ever so slightly, until the murky liquid within began to pour over the edge in a steady stream, falling into the hollow neck of the central pillar. The floating wooden balls tumbled over with it, carried on the current. The man at the crank stopped his work and leaned on the lever to watch.

Kia stood up, pressing her face to the grille to see what was happening. Her only chance in winning this game lay in understanding what was going on. Below her, in the light of the burning torches that stood in brackets all around the pit, the central pillar was filling up with water. As she watched, it began to slosh out of the lowest hole in the pillar wall; and then, a moment later, one of the floating wooden balls was carried into the hole and jammed there, plugging it. There was a heavy *click,* and Kia jumped back instinctively as the grille she was leaning against suddenly fell forward on its hinges, releasing her. On the other side of the pit, she could see Gerdi emerging, similarly freed.

There was no time to waste. Following the narrow rock path that hung in the air beneath her feet, supported only by occasional stalagmite pillars, she ran down towards the arena floor and her weapons. On either side of her, there was a fall of many meters, but she could not afford to be careful. Very soon, the water would fill up to the level when the next hole would be plugged, and somehow, she didn't think that she wanted to be defenseless when that happened.

The paths from her and Gerdi's prisons met in a central platform, standing atop a broad finger of rock. From this platform, there were several routes, all leading down. They converged at the same time, scrambling to a stop momentarily.

"Go for the weapons!" Kia instructed, and Gerdi's face showed that he had been thinking the same thing.

"When I get out of this, I'm gonna force-feed Whist to that cursed dog and then throw them *both* down the Keiko mine shaft," the younger boy promised.

"Not if I get to him first," Kia replied, choosing a path that curved steeply down and taking it. Gerdi shot off down a different one. The cheering and shouting was a constant barrage around her as her boots thumped the stone underfoot, carrying her down the precarious walkway, her red ponytail bouncing around her shoulders.

Behind her, there was another loud *click* as a wooden ball floated into place and plugged the next hole in the central pillar. She didn't know what kind of mechanism worked within that pillar, but she suspected the work of Machinists. After all, hadn't the Fallen Sun tribe built a great war-engine, the Bear Claw? A lock-release would be child's play to them.

The crowd howled in appreciation as a gate clanged open somewhere above them. Kia couldn't spare the moment it would take to see what had come out of it. She could guess, anyway. It probably wasn't called the Snapper Run for nothing. Instead, she poured on even more reckless speed, racing down the walkway towards the sandy floor of the arena, where their weapons had been left.

Behind her, she could hear something thud onto the path, and the sudden sounds of pursuit.

"Kia! It's behind you!" Gerdi shouted, from somewhere on the edge of her vision.

She jumped off the edge of the path, falling the last few feet to the ground and hitting it at a run. Ahead of her, between the forest of pillars and stalagmites that supported the upper levels, her bowstaff and Gerdi's crossbow, quiver, and shortblade were piled up loosely on the sand.

The footsteps behind her suddenly stopped, dissolving into a spring.

"Kia!" Gerdi fairly screamed.

She dived, throwing herself into a forward roll over the stack of weapons, tucking her head into her chest as she hit the sand. Her hands found her staff as she rolled over it, clasping it firmly, and she came up spinning, one end of the staff tucked under her arm and the other whipping around to meet her attacker. She caught a lightning impression of the Snapper, its overlapping jaws wide as it blurred towards her, and then she felt the nauseating crack and the jolt of the impact as her staff smashed it from the air, hitting it dead on the side of the skull. Her strike was enough to deviate the course of its dive, and it fell past her, landing in a heap. It twitched spasmodically and then fell still.

Above her, the crowd erupted in a roar of appreciation. She gave them a look of disgust. Sick vultures, getting their entertainment from death. Or was death the only entertainment, in this nightmare place?

Gerdi reached her, sliding to his knees in the sand

41

next to the Snapper and pressing his fingers under its jaw, feeling for a pulse. He looked up at Kia, his cocky grin back on his face.

"Guess he won't be needing any headache herbs," he said, then went serious. "You scared me, Kia. Be careful, huh?"

"Stop messing around," she replied brutally. "This is no time to get sentimental. Get your weapons. That pillar's filling up fast."

As if to prove her right, there was another *click* and a corresponding bellow from the mob. This time, it was more than one gate that fell open with a metallic clang. It sounded like three, all from somewhere above them. Down here, among the many pillars of various sizes that held up the plethora of arcing and looping walkways and platforms overhead, it was hard to see what was going on in the levels above.

Gerdi was throwing on his quiver of crossbow bolts and readying himself when he suddenly caught sight of something, barely visible between the thickly bunched pillars. It was only because there were torches burning on either side of it that he noticed it at all. It was a gate: a portcullis of dark, strong iron. And it was big.

A nasty sense of foreboding crept over him.

"Here they come!" Kia cried, and Gerdi rammed a

crossbow-bolt home and primed it as two Snappers dropped down from above, falling a distance that would have killed a human and landing easily on their long, spindly limbs. Gerdi sighted and fired, and his aim was good. He took one of them in the forehead, sending it to the ground in a scramble of sand. Dropping his bow, he drew his shortblade and readied himself for the other.

Wait a minute, hadn't he heard *three* gates opening?

He turned on his heel in time to see another Snapper racing towards them, dodging between the pillars, its yellowed body flashing light and dark as it ran beneath the torches.

"Kia! One behind!" he cried.

"It's yours!" she replied.

"I got it," he said, rushing out to meet it.

Kia had time to be suddenly and absurdly grateful to her father for all the years of weapons training he had put them through, before her fighting instincts took over and she engaged the Snapper. It kept a wary distance, dodging out of the way of her jabs, trying to circle her. Kia used the reach advantage that her staff provided to keep it away. It was slow, this one, slower than the Snappers they had fought in the ruins of the Forgotten Legion stockade. Maybe these ones hadn't been fed well, or were old; maybe that was why Gerdi had been able to pin one so easily with his crossbow. She didn't hold out much hope that their subsequent opponents would be the same. She suspected they would be far more vicious.

But the Snapper's caution was its downfall, for Gerdi polished off his opponent quickly and then joined Kia, his shortblade streaked with blood. Against two opponents, the lone Snapper had nowhere to run. Kia herded it towards Gerdi, and they both struck together. It almost dodged her staff, but the glancing blow she struck sent it skittering off balance, and Gerdi plunged his sword into its body. It howled and stiffened, slumping to the sand.

It had barely hit the ground before Gerdi had grabbed Kia's arm, directing her attention to the portcullis that he had seen earlier. With the howling of the crowd in their ears, conscious that the next set of gates was going to open at any second, they ran for it, Gerdi sheathing his shortblade and scooping up his crossbow as they went.

When they reached the gate, Gerdi paused, leaning against the rock wall of the pit to prime his crossbow by bracing it with his foot against the sand and pulling back the powerfully tensed string. He nocked another bolt as Kia wrapped her fingers around the bars and peered through the gaps in the portcullis, seeing only darkness within.

"Can we get out this way?" he asked urgently.

"I don't know," Kia said, wrinkling her nose at the powerful, dry, animal smell that emanated from the gate. "Do you think we —"

She was cut short by a sudden, huge movement in the darkness that made her cry out and throw herself back from the bars. Something massive had lunged at her, crashing against the portcullis and then withdrawing.

"What was *that*?" Gerdi asked, picking her up.

Kia didn't reply. Warily, she looked deep into the darkness. In the faint light, she could make out two tiny eyes, set far apart on a head fully as wide as she was tall. And she could see teeth, so many *teeth*, long and sharp, a humorless, monstrous grin. From within, something big breathed.

A sudden cold seized her. She turned to Gerdi. "You know what's gonna happen when the water reaches the top of that pillar, don't you? When the last hole is plugged."

Gerdi's young face paled. "That thing's gonna be let out," he said.

"We have to stop it," she said, pulling in vain at the metal band of the Damper Collar around her neck. "We've got to stop that from happening."

From above, there was a loud click as another hole was plugged, followed by the sound of more grilles clattering open to the cacophony of the tribe's bloodthirsty cheering.

"Come on!" Kia cried, pulling him back towards where the stone pathways wound upwards from the arena floor. They ran, their ears pricking at the sounds of scrambling above as more of the Snappers made their way down.

"Get to the pillar!" she instructed. "We have to work out how to stop it!"

She understood the Snapper Run now. As the water filled the hollow pillar, and the wooden balls plugged the holes further and further up its length, the creatures it would release would become progressively more and more difficult to defeat. And she'd wager that the topmost hole would release the beast below. They couldn't afford to let that happen. They were good fighters, both of them, but they couldn't handle something that size with the weapons they had.

They had to stop the game now, before it was too late.

Gerdi spotted one of them just as he reached the nearest upward-slanting path. It was crouched on a platform above him, its milk-white eyes glaring over the edge. He saw it a moment before it leaped, dropping like a stone towards him, its claws outstretched. He swung up his crossbow, firing with no time to aim, and then flung himself out of the way, back to the sand. The bolt glanced off the Snapper's brow, causing only a shallow flesh wound, but it was enough to stun the creature. Disoriented, its carefully controlled fall became a plummet, and it smashed into the stone walkway next to Gerdi and was still, one spindly arm swinging pathetically over the edge.

He and Kia took different routes upward, scanning the walkways above them. They could hear the clicking of the Snappers, and occasionally caught glimpses of movement, but there was no attack. These ones were careful, intelligent, and fast. They were waiting out their prey, until they had a chance to strike.

Kia had chosen a path that ran close to the central pillar, and so she took advantage of the momentary lack of action to study it. One of the plugged holes looked blankly at her, a smooth wooden ball jammed in a gap that was a tiny bit too small to let it through. The pillar was stone, and nothing they possessed was enough to damage it.

If not for these collars, this could be over in a few seconds! she thought, and felt then a frustration like she had never felt before. She had always taken her power for granted, even though the six spirit-stones in her back meant that it was particularly strong. But now that it was gone, she felt as if a part of herself was missing.

So many parts of me are missing, she thought acidly. *It's a wonder there's anything left at all.*

Glancing over her shoulder to be sure that nothing was coming after her, she jabbed her staff at the wooden ball. It pushed inward, and water gushed around it for a moment, falling into the gap between her walkway and the pillar wall; but the second she took her staff away, the wooden ball floated back to plug the hole, carried along by the rushing current. No good.

"Why aren't they coming down?" Gerdi shouted to her, from where he stood on another path. He'd re-nocked his crossbow and was aiming up at where he could hear the Snappers, but he was unable to get a shot.

The crowd was chanting impatiently, obviously unimpressed with the Snappers' tactics. The tribesman who was working the crank gave it another pull, tautening the rope and tipping the huge wooden vat a fraction more. The water sluiced out a little more vigorously.

Kia looked up hatefully at the crank-man, and then her eyes suddenly widened in realization.

"They're stalling us!" she shouted to Gerdi. "They're waiting till the next set of gates opens!"

Gerdi swore under his breath. That meant they would have to go up there and get them.

There was another *click*, and another hole was plugged.

"Go!" Kia yelled, and they ran up their respective paths, heading for the upper levels.

The Snappers screeched as they saw their prey rushing towards them, drowning out the sound of grilles falling open. They came racing down to meet the attack. Gerdi looked around frantically, trying to catch sight of the new arrivals to the arena, but he was foiled by the chaos of walkways around him.

Kia reached a wide, uneven platform and planted herself there, waiting for Gerdi to reach her. If there was anywhere to make a stand, it was here. Although four paths branched off from it at odd angles — two up, two down — it was better than trying to face the agile Snappers on one of the narrow walkways, where they were just as likely to fall to their deaths as to be killed by the creatures.

The Snappers hissed, disappointed that their prey had chosen defensible ground, but their blood was up, and their patience had run out. They came scampering down, four of them now, coming from all directions. Kia looked up at the central pillar, and her heart froze. There was only one more hole to plug. Then the beast would be out.

"The rope!" she shouted. "Gerdi! Get the rope!"

And then the Snappers were on them. Kia yelled a battle cry as she met the first, lashing at it with her staff. She caught a lucky strike, taking it off guard in midstep, and it squealed as it flailed the air before dropping off the walkway. But a second one was on her, scuttling along a different path and launching itself over Gerdi, crashing into her back and knocking her down to the floor. She felt her head roughly pulled back by the hair, exposing her throat, and then Gerdi's sword swept down and she felt the hot, wet splash of blood on her back. The creature slumped off her, beheaded.

"Keep them off me!" he shouted, scooping up his crossbow, which he had dropped, and Kia rushed to stand between him and the two remaining Snappers.

Through the walkways and platforms above him, he could see the thick black line of the rope that was attached to the vat of water, pulled tight by the crank. He heard the clash of wood on bone as Kia and the Snappers met. Bracing himself, taking a breath, he took aim. The fight next to him was a distraction he couldn't afford. A bead of sweat trickled into his eye; he blinked it away.

The murky water had nearly filled to the top hole. A wooden ball bobbed on the surface of the liquid, waiting to be carried into the gap and plug it, releasing the creature below.

"Okay, Gerdi," he muttered to himself. "You're always mouthing off about how good you are. Now's time to prove it."

Closing one eye, he fired.

Kia slammed into him, knocked backward by a vicious strike from her assailants. The crossbow fell out of his hands, clattering to the stone. Stumbling under Kia's weight, he managed to pull his shortblade out, a moment before they both crashed to the ground, Gerdi pinned under Kia. And as the Snapper leaped for the kill, he thrust it out under Kia's armpit, feeling the jolt as the Snapper buried itself onto the length of steel and the steaming spray of sticky blood that spattered them both.

"Get off!" he cried, wriggling beneath both Kia and the corpse of the Snapper. The crowd above were screaming and yelling their approval; but over it all, Gerdi could tell that the sound of the water tumbling into the pillar had not stopped. They were perhaps seconds away from the release of the beast.

In that moment of urgency, it seemed as if Gerdi was possessed, filled with a strength that he did not know he had. He shoved his way free of Kia, hefting her and the deadweight of the Snapper as if they were nothing. He got to his feet at a run, his shortblade flashing out as the last Snapper scampered towards him, its beaklike mouth open in a squeal of fury. Without breaking stride, he feinted a swing to the ribs and at the last moment angled the blade upwards, driving it under the Snapper's jaw right up to the hilt and then planting his foot in its chest, kicking it away.

It stumbled backwards and toppled over the edge of the platform, Gerdi's blade still lodged in it; but Gerdi was already grabbing his crossbow, pulling a bolt from his quiver, and running, seeking a good angle for a shot at the rope. His first shot had missed narrowly, or nicked the edge; he couldn't see. This would be his last chance.

With the yells and cheers of the tribesmen swamping his brain, he stopped halfway up one of the paths, braced the crossbow against his foot, and loaded it. He swung it upward, fitting it to his shoulder, closing one eye as he took aim.

All or nothing.

He fired, feeling the buck of the catch as the bolt was loosed . . .

. . . and the onlookers exploded into celebration as the bolt sheared through the rope, snapping the vat free. It rocked back in its stone cradle, returning to its upright position, the final few inches of water that would have filled the pillar to the last hole stored safely within its wooden body.

Gerdi's face split into a broad grin. He felt an elation such as he had never known sweep through his body. Ropes came snaking down the sides of the pit, and Kia rushed up behind him to gather him in a hug, lifting him off the ground. He hugged her back. Somehow, there was a feeling of a test passed here, a trial endured. It was in the tone of the tribesmen. Their cheers were no longer malicious, but almost comradely. Had this been all some kind of initiation?

They walked exhaustedly to where there was a platform up against the pit wall, and there grabbed the ropes that had been thrown down to them. Half climbing, half hauled, they ascended the sides of the pit, and many hands were there to help them over the lip and into the cheering throng. Their backs were battered under pats of congratulation, and meaningless words swarmed around them, spoken by unknown faces.

But suddenly, one voice came to Kia's ear, calling her name. It was unmistakable. Hardly daring to believe her senses, her eyes welled with tears. And then, pushing through the crowd, there came a face that she recognized. His hair had been shorn off, and his face and skin were painted in the same manner as the rest of the tribe; but his eyes, that nose, that mouth . . .

It was Ty.

She threw herself into him, and they encircled each other in a desperate hug. And for the first time since the day she lost him, Kia cried and cried.

Broken Sky

Act One
Part Eight

Broken Sky

TY

KETTIN

THE BEAR CLAW

1

Loose of Their Cages

"Sit down, please," Ty offered, and she did.

His quarters were a spartan affair, a round room at the top of a short, stumpy two-story tower of hastily laid bricks and wood. There was little in it but a sleeping pallet, a stone washbasin, and a wide, jagged piece of polished metal that was used as a mirror. There was also a narrow fireplace, in which embers still smoldered, and a roughly carved chair before it. The ceiling was high, the rafters disappearing in the darkness above; the floorboards creaked underfoot.

But none of this interested Kia as she sat down on the edge of the pallet. She was watching only Ty, as he crouched with his back to her, stirring up the fire and feeding it fresh fuel. His appearance had changed so much. His unkempt, wild black hair was gone. His narrow shoulders and bare arms were now corded with lean muscle. He no longer wore simple stable garments, but hard-wearing boots and a motley assortment of whatever he had been able to scavenge together to clothe himself.

He finished stoking the fire and drew the chair up in front of her, then sat down, too. For a long while, they just looked at each other; she with her dirtied and beautiful face under a tangle of red hair, he with his drastically new appearance, one side red and one side blue. Finally, it was Ty who spoke.

"You came to find me?" he said, his voice not as strong as he might have liked.

Kia smiled, her eyes still raw from the long-overdue tears she had shed. "Yeah," she said.

"Thanks."

"S'okay."

A pause. They both looked at their knees awkwardly.

"It's good to see you," she said at last.

"I'm glad . . . you got out. Of Osaka Stud."

"I thought you were dead," she replied.

"I know. So did I." He smiled weakly. "The stables collapsed after they blew out the hub. But I was right on the rim, in the lock-chamber. They built it pretty sturdily, I guess. But still, most of it fell down on me." He looked into the greenness of her irises. "They dug me out. Some of their Guardsmen were trapped inside, and they found me by accident. They figured I wasn't dead yet, so they put me with the captives. That's how I got here."

"Oh, Ty, I'm *sorry*," Kia blurted. "We left you. We left you behind."

He took her hands in his, touching her as he had never dared do before. "Hey, it's okay. Why do you think I lied to you about where Banto was? I knew you'd never leave otherwise. *I'm* sorry. I'm sorry I had to deceive you."

"I knew you lied," she said, her voice quiet. "I think, even then, I knew you were lying."

She hung her head, reeling under the barrage of emotions that had seeped through the chinks in her armour at the sight of him. It was Ty's voice that she heard — it was so *good* to hear — but it was infused with a new confidence, a new strength now. No longer was he the shy, unsure boy that she had left behind; and yet he *was*, still, tender and sweet and sensitive underneath.

She shuddered, flinching under the sudden rush of an emotion she did not recognize. She pulled her hands away from his, and was strangely gratified to see him drop them hastily, as if he thought he'd gone too far, overstepped his boundaries.

"What happened?" she asked, more out of the need to say something than the need to know anything specific. She let him make up his own mind what she meant.

"They questioned me," he said, leaning back, his face disappearing into shadow. "I told them what I knew. Then they . . . questioned me some more."

"What did you know?" Kia asked.

"Nothing," he replied. "Did you?"

"I didn't then. I do now," she replied.

"So do I," he answered, letting his voice trail off. Then he seemed to come back to himself. "Anyway, when they were done, they took me to Os Dakar. I think they were going to execute me, because you and I had been . . ." He paused, then finished: "Friends." He looked at her, his eyes nervously roaming her features. "But at the last minute, an order came through. I was told it was from Macaan himself. So they didn't kill me. They sent me here instead."

"You seem like a hero here," Kia ventured. "With the Bear Claw, surely the tribe needs you more than —"

"I'm a *killer* here!" he snapped, suddenly standing

up, his chair falling over behind him. Kia's eyes mirrored her shock. He turned away, unable to bear the wounded look there, and walked to stand in front of the fire, silhouetted against the light.

"I'm sorry," he said at last. "At times, I almost get used to it. I accept it, y'know? I mean, I've been here long enough to pick up the lingo, the crazy speech they talk, but . . ." He hunkered down in front of the fire. "Here I'm accepted. Here they need me. They like me. They have respect for me. More than they ever would for someone who's only been here a few months. Sometimes I think I'm one of them." He turned around, and his eyes were a dark glimmer in his painted face. "And then something happens, like you, and I remember what I used to be, and what I've become."

"What *have* you become?" Kia asked.

"A murderer," he replied. "I live, I earn my place in this tribe, by driving the Bear Claw. Kia, if you could *see* what it *does* to people . . ." His shoulders sagged. "You shouldn't have come for me," he said. "I'm not what you remember."

"You *are* what I remember," she said, getting to her feet and pacing restlessly. "You think you're the only one who's been changed by this? I have . . . *such* a *hate* inside me. A hatred for Macaan, for the Guardsmen, for everything and everyone that killed my father. I let it go in Tusami City. In a crowded market. Cetra knows how many innocents I might have killed, if it had gone another way." She stopped, her hands gripping the side of her hair. "But I killed those Guardsmen. I've done that much. And if you're a murderer, that makes me a murderer, too."

"You're not a murderer," Ty said, quietly insistent. "Not you. It was self-defense."

"It *wasn't* self-defense, Ty," Kia replied stridently. "It was *war*. I didn't ask to be part of it, and neither did you. But both of us have had to kill to stay alive. That's the game Macaan has brought us into. And if either of us hadn't done what we had to, I wouldn't be standing here and you wouldn't have lasted two days in this place."

She let the weight of her words settle in the silence that followed them. Then she spoke again, her voice softer.

"Ty, we didn't want to be made into what we are. We both want things to be like they were before. But that's gone now, all of it. We have to go on."

Another long silence, broken only by the snapping of the growing fire. When next Ty spoke, he changed the subject entirely, not wishing to think about what she had said.

"We found your friends, too."

Kia swiveled urgently. "You'd better not have put *them* through what me and Gerdi —"

"No, it's okay," he said. "Whist told us where he had left the rest of the newcomers; that was as much as I knew when I went along. I recognized Elani and Ryushi when we got there. I told the party that had been sent to capture them that they were friends of mine. I talked to Elani. She told me where you'd gone, and I came right back. A little late, I guess."

"I'm still here," she said.

"They put all the newcomers in the Snapper Run," he said apologetically. "Whist keeps an eye out for fresh arrivals, and brings them to Kettin, the tribal captain. If they beat the Snapper Run, they're allowed to join the tribe."

"What if they don't want to?" Kia asked.

"Nobody says no," Ty replied. "Look around you, Kia. You think you'd survive here on your own? Even Whist, for all his talking about being independent, has to rely on us to some extent."

"But why all the charade? Why go to all the trouble of breaking in?"

63

"It's Whist's thing," Ty said. "He has to prove to himself that he can get in and out whenever he wants. Kettin humors him and turns a blind eye to it. He's good, though. He always manages to lead people to us without a fight."

"Yeah, I noticed," said Kia, remembering the trap he had sprung on her. "So where are the others, anyway?"

"They're in quarters. They're my guests. Kettin gives me a lot of privileges like that, in return for . . . what I do for him. That's how I got those Damper Collars taken off you and Gerdi, to start with."

"Can I see them? Ryushi and the others."

"We have to talk first," Ty replied. It wasn't really a request. The old Ty would never have spoken like that; but then, the old Ty, like a lot of things, had changed. He got up from the fire and walked over to her, so that they stood face-to-face in the growing warmth of the room. "Kia, listen. This is important. They took me places, when they were questioning me. I saw and heard things, things I didn't really understand then, but now I do."

"I don't —"

"*Listen*," he hissed, and then, gentler: "Please, Kia. This might be the only chance I get to tell you this, and someone has to know. A lot of people come to Os Dakar, from the Dominions and from Kirin Taq. A lot of people, from a lot of places, who've seen things like I have. Maybe it's only because we're all gathered here, that only we seem to be able to see the whole picture. But we're the only people who can't do anything *about* it."

He turned away, walked over to the fire, and stared into it once again, as if, within its flames, he could find the words he needed.

"Do you have a way to get out of here?" he asked.

"Yeah," she replied.

"Then promise me that, whatever happens to me, you'll get away to get this information to the people who can use it."

"No."

His shaven head half turned, paused. "No?"

"I've left too many people behind," she said. "I've lost too many. I'm not doing it again, Ty. It hurts too much." She walked over and stood next to him, staring into the heart of the fire as he did. "I promise you that I'm not leaving Os Dakar without you, and that's the only way I *am* going. That's the best you'll get from me."

She expected an argument from him, but he gave her none. "You always did know your own mind," he said, his voice curving into a smile.

"I did," she said. "I'd like to again, one day."

Her words seemed to fall dead as they came from her

65

mouth. The fire crackled noisily. The rafters above them were half-seen cross-beams spanning a pit of shadow.

"After Macaan had ordered me taken to Os Dakar," Ty said, "they took me to a Ley Warren. That's what they called it. It's like . . . it's like that one time, when we went out really far from the Stud, and there was that valley. You remember?"

"I remember."

"And when we were there, we saw that termite colony? Those big towers of solid earth, taller than we were, six or seven of them of different heights and shapes, all linked together? We called it the City of the Termites, remember? And we couldn't believe that things so small could make something so huge."

"Yeah," said Kia with a smile. How strange, that she had been thinking of exactly the same event when she had formulated the plan to get into Os Dakar. "It seems a long time ago."

"This Ley Warren," he continued. "That was what it was like. Except it was as if *I* were the termite, the *size* of a termite in comparison. And inside it, everywhere . . . Keriags. Thousands upon thousands of them. They're hiding them in there. The Guardsmen on the outside keep people out, while the Keriags build from the inside up."

Kia felt a rill of repulsion run across her face as she thought of the black, shiny skins of the insectile Keriags.

"I don't know how many of those things work under Macaan, but I know there are at least seven of those Ley Warrens, from what people here have told me. They're all over the Dominions. But that's not all. They're all over Kirin Taq as well."

Something that Calica had said before they left Gar Jenna, relayed to her by Ryushi during the few times they had spoken, blinked across Kia's mind: It had to do with strange constructions that had recently appeared at certain regions in the Dominions.

"What are they?" she asked.

"I don't know," he replied. "I was taken there to meet a Resonant; I think it was one Macaan had newly captured. He took me over to Kirin Taq, so I could be transported to Os Dakar."

Kia frowned. "But why would he send you here?" she mused to herself.

"That's not everything," Ty continued. "Kettin, the leader of the Fallen Sun . . . his brother was a Resonant. He was one of the first to be taken when Macaan started rounding them up."

"To the Ley Warrens?" Kia asked. "Is *that* where they're being taken?"

Ty nodded, his newly unfamiliar face washed by the firelight. "Kettin followed them, and led a group in to try and get his brother out. He was one of the best thieves there was. King Macaan himself was staying there, in temporary quarters, overseeing . . . whatever it was they were doing. Kettin went in there to get his brother, but he couldn't resist the chance of seeing what he could get from the King's quarters." He smiled faintly. "I guess he's always been a thief at heart. Anyway, Kettin was captured, along with the rest of them; but not before he'd stolen King Macaan's own earring from where it lay on his dressing table. He says that if Macaan had been there he could've killed him and been done with it all." Ty paused. "He never found his brother. He was sent to Os Dakar. He managed to hide the earring by swallowing it. He wears it still."

But Kia jerked around at his words, sudden realization on her face. She grabbed him by the shoulders. In the polished-metal mirror above the washbasin, reflected figures moved in synchronicity.

"Macaan's *earring*? And it is really his? Ty, if we could get that, we could find out *everything*!"

"What? How?"

Kia tried to calm her mounting excitement, but she was still speaking breathlessly. "Calica, back at Gar

Jenna. She's psychometric. She can tell the past from touching an object. That earring might have been worn by Macaan all the time he was planning this. If we can get it to her . . . we'll know everything!"

"Are you sure?"

"It's a chance!"

"He'll never part with it."

"Then we'll take it off him!"

Now it was Ty's turn to grip her shoulders, steadying her firmly. His eyes, once so soft, now bored into her.

"Kia, stop."

She stopped, chastened. Having kept her emotions under such strict rein for so long, she was embarrassed to find them raging uncontrollably within her, like long-penned beasts that had broken loose of their cages. When she had quieted, her face tilted expectantly, he spoke.

"I can't leave this place," he said, and then raised a hand to hush her as she drew breath to protest. "They'll never let me go. The Fallen Sun were just another tribe until Whist found me. They'd been waiting for a Pilot for months. The Bear Claw was already built. But now, with me, they're the strongest. They can rule this island. They can make it safe, regulate it, turn Os Dakar from a war zone into one big tribe. It's Kettin's dream: to make Os

Dakar whole. We can do it in secret; nobody ever checks what goes on here. Once we all work together, neither Macaan nor Princess Aurin can hold us in."

"You sound like you agree with him," Kia said flatly.

"I agree with the principle. Not the method."

"Because you're still a murderer. In your own eyes."

Ty released her, as if unwilling to touch her after she had dealt him such a cruel reminder. It seemed her ability to wound had not entirely deserted her upon finding Ty at last.

"It is a foolish man who rages against what he cannot change," he said quietly.

"Muachi, right? The philosopher?"

"Right."

"You remember the day Father died, you told me about The Game? That was Muachi, too. The Game of Man and Woman."

"You said that you didn't know it," Ty replied, recalling it as if it were yesterday. "I said you wouldn't play by the rules if you did."

"That's right, I wouldn't play by the rules," she said. "But I never said I wouldn't *play*."

And with those words, the final barriers between them collapsed, the fear that each of them held of allowing another to care for them, and they met in a kiss that had the force of years behind it, as if it had long been destined to happen but had only now been allowed to. They kissed each other desperately, dissolving into one another, and Ty knew that he could not live without Kia now, and she knew that she would risk anything to take him with her from this place, and tears fell from both of them as, finally, their scarred souls began to heal.

From where he hid in the rafters, Whist watched, digesting all that he had heard, arranging it for Kettin's ears.

From behind the polished-metal mirror, unseen by the two figures entwined before the fire or the one that hid in the shadows, a telescopic brass eyepiece whirred, focusing.

2

Much Prey Tonight

"Goodgreet, tribe-brother Ty," said Mila, her weathered face creasing into a smile as she saw him. Once, she had been pretty, a Harvest Queen of a small Dominion village. Then she had fallen for the wrong man, a traitor to the King. When he had been caught and executed, she had been implicated and imprisoned. Her time on Os Dakar had ravaged her beauty with strife and battle, and buried it under the painted halves of the Fallen Sun's tribal colors. The sheen of her silver-blue hair had faded; but when she smiled, a glimmer of what had once been showed through.

"Goodgreet, Mila," Ty replied. "Is tribe-captain Kettin inside, nai?"

They were standing outside Kettin's quarters, a three-story building with the lowest floor made of stone and the upper two constructed of lighter wood. A balcony jutted out above them, overhanging; a sentry stood at each corner, watching the surrounding camp. Nothing could get close without being seen.

But Ty was known here, and he wore the tribal colors, and so he had walked under the unwavering gaze of the sentries and up to the door — a thick wooden affair that hung slightly off-angle due to poor workmanship on the hinges — and up to Mila, Kettin's door-sentry ever since Ty arrived, and long before. Torches rippled flame in their brackets, lightening the permanent dimness of Kirin Taq.

"Kettin's inside, rightsome," she replied. "But not to be eyemet. He's asleep."

Asleep, Ty thought. *Good*. His hand, hanging by his side, flicked a sign to the one who was watching, unnoticed by Mila.

"Are you suretain?" Ty asked, effortlessly speaking the curious, hybrid language of the Fallen Sun, with which they recognized each other. Each tribe had a different variation on the language, and whereas tribal colors could be painted on to anyone, learning each tribe's oddities of dialect was an altogether harder matter for impostors to accomplish. "I eyemet him only just, and we arranged to be meeting here."

"True? But he never takes leave without telling me."

"Lessly he parted by the sentry's rung-ladder, nai?" Ty suggested. To prevent the sentries from coming in and out through Kettin's quarters all the time to get to their posts on the first-floor balcony, a rough log ladder leaned against one side. The first-floor wind-holes (there was no glass on Os Dakar) could provide easy access to the balcony.

"Think you?" Mila began, but then caught sight of who was approaching over Ty's shoulder, and relaxed. "Ah! Eyethere. Kettin."

Ty looked around, and saw the twelve-winter, green-haired boy who was Gerdi walking across the torchlit, stony clearing towards him. But then, Gerdi wasn't trying to make *him* see Kettin in the place of that young boy; only those sentries that observed him, and Mila. His face was set, concentrating. It was a difficult task, to work on manipulating the perception of several people like that, even to one as practiced as he was.

He walked up and stood next to Ty. Mila opened the door for him, frowning. "Tribe-captain Kettin. You'd betterly tell me each leavetime."

She was politely berating him for not informing her when he had left his quarters. After all, she had a job to do.

"Be forgivesome," Kettin-Gerdi replied, his voice coming out deep and strong like the older man. Now that he had passed beneath the balcony, and out of the view of the sentries, he could concentrate solely on Mila.

Mila was a little offended by his curt manner, and that she had not been offered an explanation; but she let him by, and Ty with him, assuming that he had had something to drink or was feeling bad. She closed the door behind them, and resumed her post, a little perturbed by the unusual event but convinced that everything was all right now.

Shut away from sight, Ty and Gerdi relaxed for a moment. Smokeless torches burned around them, illuminating a heavy table covered with scraps of food, a few chairs, and a fireplace with no chimney. A set of stone steps led to the wooden upper stories.

"She'd better be right," Gerdi said quietly. "If he's not asleep, we'll be in a *world* o' trouble."

He didn't really expect an answer, and Ty didn't give him one.

They headed stealthily up the stairs, careful not to make any noise. Gerdi kept up his illusion in case one of the sentries should happen to look in one of the wind-holes as they crossed the first-floor room to the upper sleeping-quarters; but the sentries all had their backs turned, facing outward, and didn't hear a thing. Stepping carefully between the discarded debris that Kettin had left lying around, they softly ascended to the upper level.

There were no wind-holes here, and the torches had been extinguished; but as they poked their heads up through the hatch, the light from below them traced the outlines of the features of the room. A chest, a set of keys, a sleeping-pallet piled with blankets; and hunched under it, the sleeping form of Kettin.

Ty stayed where he was. Quietly, on cat feet, Gerdi crossed the room, treading lightly on the floorboards, until he was standing next to the pallet. Luck was with them; he was lying on his side, his earring-ear up. Gerdi looked at the silver ornament, a thin band speckled with tiny white diamonds. Rubbing his fingers together, he reached for it, to separate the clasp on either side and draw it from the sleeping ear. . . .

"That would be wiseless," Kettin spoke, and Gerdi jumped back in alarm. A moment later, he heard the sound of thumping footsteps downstairs, and Ty was pushed roughly up and into the room. A torch was brought, and rested in a wall-sconce. In moments, they were surrounded.

Kettin levered himself up from his bed, looked at them as if they were errant puppies, and sighed wearily. He had a broad face, and a squashed, broken nose, but other than that his bald head and skin colors conformed to the patterns of the tribe. When he spoke, his teeth flashed between his lips, and they were crooked and browned. His eyes were the white of the Kirins, but without his skin coloring or hair visible, it was otherwise impossible to tell him from Dominion-folk. Perhaps, Gerdi realized, that was one reason why they went to so much trouble to paint themselves. Kirins or Dominion-folk; they were all the same here. Hochi might benefit from a little of that philosophy, he mused.

"Bring them withly," Kettin said to his guards, his tone suggesting the depressing predictability of the theft. He was still fully dressed under his blankets, and he walked past them and down the stairs, sparing them not even a glance. The guards, holding them by the arms with the hooked ends of their tribal bola a hair's breadth from their napes, manhandled them after him. Nobody spoke.

They were taken to a clearing, a sort of gathering place that had sprung up in the gap left between two clusters of erratic housing. The ever-present torches burned all around, brightening the endless twilight, and a good portion of the tribe was gathered there, waiting in a wide ring on the stony ground.

By now, Ty had realized that their plan had been anticipated; what he did not expect to see were Kia and the others, standing in the center of the clearing under the watchful eyes of more tribesmen and women.

Elani watched him appear, brought through the mob towards them. She was holding herself under control, trying to quell the fear that swelled inside her. She had been told of the plan, like the others. But almost as soon as Ty and Gerdi had left, the tribesmen had arrived to grab them. Even Kia and Ryushi couldn't fight all these men and women; after all, the tribespeople had spirit-stones, too. It would be so easy for everyone to gather together, for her to shift, bring them all into the safety of the Dominions and away from Os Dakar. But they didn't have the *earring*, and Kia had gone to great pains to explain how important that was. As if she needed telling.

So she waited, a maturity born of years of hardship keeping her childish panic under a lid.

"They had nothing to —" Ty began to protest to Kettin as he saw them, but a sharp elbow in the back of his head silenced him brutally.

He and Gerdi were shoved over to join the others, and then the guards retreated to a distance. They stood there for a minute, enduring the gazes of the surrounding mob. Most of them were centered on Ty, the only spot of red-and-blue in an island of strangers; the looks were a blend of hate, suspicion, and puzzlement.

Then Kettin stepped up to them, and with him came a familiar figure, accompanied by his huge, loping grey dog. Ty stepped forward to the front of them, to meet his leader. Kia's eyes flickered nervously over his back.

"Whist told me this could happen, nai?" Kettin said, his voice loud enough so they could all hear. "That tribe-brother Ty's friends could regrab him from us. I disbetrusted him. Not Pilot Ty, I told him. Nai." He turned his gaze away from Ty, raking it over the assembled others. Elani quailed, sniffing back frightened tears, burrowing closer to Ryushi. "But eyemeet him now, our Pilot. Caught in the event of attrying to murder me as I slept."

Nobody argued the charge. It was pointless. It didn't make any difference. Besides, they wouldn't have been heard over the roar of indignation and anger that erupted from the mob. Kettin paced before them, his feet crunching gravel. Behind him, the eclipsed sun of Kirin Taq presided over them with disinterest. Suddenly, he leaned in closer to Ty.

"But faithloyal Whist told me something else, too," he hissed, so only Ty could hear. "Your friends have a way off Os Dakar, nai?"

Ty looked blandly past him at Whist, the young, lean boy with the crazy multicolor hair. His gaze was returned with an expression that said: *We all do what we gotta do.*

"Now tribe-brother Ty underknows," Kettin said, raising his voice to the mob and swiveling with a magnanimous gesture, "that he is the solely one that can driverate the mashsmashing Bear Claw. And without the Bear Claw, the Fallen Sun cannot continue our goodly work, nai? He under*knows* we cannot murder him as he wouldly murder me." There was a pause, and then a grin spread across his face, displaying his crooked teeth. "But we can murder his friends, nai?"

"Kill them and I'll never drive for you again," Ty growled over the new tumult of approval from the mob, purposely using his usual Dominion-speech instead of the mangled grammar of the Fallen Sun.

"Then we murder them onely by onely," replied Kettin. "Every waketime. Until we murder a friend you care about *realsome*."

His eyes flicked to Kia, then back to Ty, letting him know that he knew. Ty's face tightened.

"Unless we tell you about how we're to get off Os Dakar?" Ty said. The crowd's cries had died now, but their conversation was still only audible to those right next to them. Blink snuffed in the background, then began to worry at an itch in his haunch.

"Unless," Kettin agreed.

"So you can leave, take a few of your closest with you?" Ty asked.

Kettin grinned. "You underestimate me. All the Fallen Sun, Pilot Ty. All the Fallen Sun are my closest. Even faithloyal Whist and his dog."

Whist, who had crouched to pat Blink, looked up at Ty with an odd smile. Ty ignored him, his gaze locked with Kettin's.

"You made me a murderer," he said.

"Murder is a way of life on Os Dakar. I'm attrying to change that."

"But you're willing to run away, to get off this place, if you get the chance."

"You have your friends, I have mine. We leavetake if we can. Betterly for the Fallen Sun."

The crowd were stirring impatiently now, eager to know what Kettin intended to do with the prisoners, craning to hear their private conversation. Ty and Kettin faced each other, almost palpable tension crackling between them. If Ty told Kettin how they intended to get off Os Dakar, they would become expendable. They wouldn't even need the Bear Claw anymore. He and his friends would almost certainly be killed for his crime against the Fallen Sun. He knew how these things worked; he'd seen it before.

Matters were complicated by the fact that he didn't *know* how Kia intended to get them off the plateau; she hadn't told him. But it was his one and only lever in this debate, and he had to try and bluff until he could come up with something better.

The crowd finally fell silent, the quiet radiating outward from where Ty and Kettin locked wills, his dark blue eyes linked with Kettin's cream-on-white. Nothing stirred. Even the wind seemed to die.

And then, faintly, came a noise. At first, it was the tiniest buzz on the edge of their consciousness, a sound without definition and near-unnoticeable. Then it began to take shape. One by one, the sharpest ears in the crowd turned their heads unconsciously, noting it. A rapid, staccato tapping; many rhythms overlapping into a frenzied jumble. Now they could all hear it, and Kettin broke off from Ty to turn towards its source. But it didn't seem to *have* a source; it was coming from all around them. Louder and louder. Inexorable. Unstoppable.

"*Keriags!*" one of the sentries yelled. "*Thousands* of *Keriags!*"

For a second, everything was frozen. No, it was *impossible*, Kettin thought. There were no Keriags on Os Dakar, except those few that acted as sentries. They were the shock troops of the Princess Aurin, not indigenous scavengers like the Snappers. Why would they be here? They *couldn't* be here.

He turned back to the prisoners with a look of naked hate.

Unless the Keriags had come for *them*.

The second was over, and the stockade burst into pandemonium. The renowned discipline of the Fallen Sun collapsed in a shambles. The crowd scattered in all directions, half of them heading to man the wall defenses, half of them fleeing aimlessly in panic. The other tribes on Os Dakar, those they could handle. But there were not more than two hundred in the whole of the Fallen Sun tribe, and each Keriag was worth five men at least. They were many times outnumbered.

The prisoners were forgotten in the sudden rush, and Hochi tried to sweep up Elani protectively in his arms as tribesmen shoved and jostled past them, a blurred sea of red and blue. But he was too slow; someone fell into her, and she was crushed underneath them. The tribesman scrambled off her and ran, heedless of what he had done; but when Hochi scooped Elani up, he saw with horror that her black hair was wet with blood, and her eyes were closed. In the same instant, Ty leaped on Kettin, who was glaring in disbelief at the chaos all around him, and bore him to the ground. Kettin fell badly, winding himself; and as he struggled for breath, his Kirin eyes bulging, Ty hooked two fingers around his earring and pulled it roughly from his ear, tearing a bloody path through his lobe. Kettin tried to howl, but his breath was locked in his chest, and he could only gasp as Ty stole the hooking-flail from his belt and ran with his prize, shouting for the others to follow him as he disappeared out of the torchlight.

Somewhere, the Keriags had reached the stockade walls. The Fallen Sun tribe had similar fortifications to those of the Forgotten Legion, with cruel, uneven spikes jutting outward at angles that supposedly made a direct assault impossible. Not for the Keriags, though. Their six long, spiderlike, knob-kneed legs were armoured with a horny black chitin, and they simply sped up the walls, using the jagged edges as footholds. Their bodies, cradled between their legs, weaved around the spikes, their forelimbs clutching their *gaer bolga*. The best defenses in Os Dakar were no defense against a Keriag, and they scuttled up and over the fortifications as easily as if they were flat ground. Ty heard the screaming begin as the first of the creatures made its slaughterous path inward.

"Where are we going?" Kia yelled at Ty over the sounds of panic.

"The escape tunnel's over that way!" Gerdi cried, pointing away across the camp.

"Let Kettin take the tunnel. I'll bet my life the Keriags have already found it, somehow," Ty said grimly. "We're going for the Bear Claw."

But he didn't have time to voice the terrible understanding that had suddenly presented itself to him. Why here? Why now, that the Keriags attacked? And then it had all made sense, why Macaan had ordered him kept alive and sent to Os Dakar instead of being executed. Because the King knew that Kia and Ryushi would come for their friend, if they knew he was here; and he had undoubtedly spread the word widely enough so that Parakkan spies could not fail to come across it.

The Jachyra had been keeping a watch on him the whole time, waiting for the children of the traitor to turn up so the Keriags could kill them.

"What about El? Is she alright?" Ryushi asked Hochi, who bore her in his massive arms.

"I don't know," he muttered, looking at the unconscious child, cradled against his chest. "I don't know."

They ran onward, ignored by the tribesmen now, just another part of the nightmarish madness that had suddenly swooped on their world. The air was thickening with the sounds of combat and the cries of those who fell before the silent killers that were swarming into the stockade. The shambolic huts and buildings swept past on either side of them, meaningless, leaning in closely as if to hem them up as they dodged from torchlight to shadow, torchlight to shadow.

And then, suddenly, there it was. Nestled between two storage sheds, grey under the faint light of Kirin Taq's sun: the Bear Claw.

It was huge, a towering monstrosity of blackened iron and oil, of pipes and pistons. Rising high above them, it brooded in its own blackness, like a sleeping behemoth waiting to be roused. If it could have been said to have a shape, it would have been vaguely cylindrical; but the innumerable protrusions — spikes, juts, cupolas, bladed fins — rendered any kind of symmetry impossible. It squatted between two enormous caterpillar tracks, humping up on either side like shoulders. It was, like everything else on Os Dakar, a bizarre assemblage of whatever materials and ideas had been at hand at the time. Some things, like the heat-exhaust pipes that bristled along its back, had an obvious purpose. Most things did not, occupying a strange position between protection and ornamentation, and making the whole vast beast seem like a scrappy, but nevertheless fearsome, clutter of junk.

Their moment of awe was destroyed by a terrible, bellowing howl that slit the sky around them, echoing like a thunderclap across Os Dakar. Kia's spine froze, and she was struck by an awful realization. The thing, the creature that had been kept at the bottom of the Snapper Run, the one that had almost bitten her arm off through its gate. Someone had released it. The monster was out.

"Come on!" Ty yelled, urging them onward.

They ran into the shadow of the massive Machinist vehicle, their feet crunching the loose gravel beneath them, following Ty to where a set of rungs, jutting from the side of the Bear Claw, led up to the wide roof. So intent were they on their destination that they almost did not hear that their footsteps were suddenly being punctuated by a higher, clicking tap, rapidly approaching. But then Tochaa swung around, his terse bark of alarm alerting the others, and they looked back to see a pair of Keriags skitter from behind a dangerously listing two-story building and fix them with their black eyes.

"Get up there! Go!" Ryushi shouted at Ty, shoving him towards the rungs. "Start it up. We'll hold them off."

Ty hesitated for a moment, his gaze flicking to Kia, who was weaponless like the rest of them; only he was armed, and Kettin's hooking-flail would be useless to anyone but him. Still, he saw the sense in what Ryushi said, and he wasted no more than an instant on indecision before he threw himself up the rungs and began clambering to the top.

Ryushi glanced back at the child Elani, held in Hochi's arms, a thin ribbon of blood trailing from her hairline. There would be more Keriags here any moment; he could hear the approach of the hordes that clambered over the ineffective defenses of the stockade. If she was hurt, hurt badly . . . then there was no chance for them. All their prayers of escape were invested in that little girl, the Resonant. If she didn't recover soon, they could not hope to hold out, even with the formidable powers they wielded between them.

"Hochi! Try and wake her!" Kia ordered, sharing Ryushi's thoughts. She had not lost the tone of command that she had acquired over her time in Gar Jenna.

If it sounded a little cruel and callous, she couldn't help that now. Their lives were on the line, and perhaps the lives of everyone in the Dominions, if they couldn't get King Macaan's earring to Parakka. She turned back to the approaching danger. "I'll handle these."

The Keriags came towards them, their spindly legs tapping the ground urgently, the jagged sides of their *gaer bolga* catching the torchlight. Kia's head bowed, her eyes closed; and suddenly the stones in her back flared dark red, and the Keriags' onward progress was brutally arrested by an earthen pair of hands, which darted out of the solid ground and gripped on to the hindmost leg of each of them. Surprised, they were not quick enough to avoid being trapped in the crushing grip, but they reacted to their predicament with inhuman speed, instantly turning the edges of their spears to hack at their restraints.

But the ground here was tough and stony, and it did not yield easily under their strikes. Instead, the rest of the golem began to slowly form out of the ground, Kia bringing it up, shaping it, as if it were ascending on a platform out of the solid earth. First the forearms that supported the strong hands; then the chest, with the golem's crude face set deep within it; and then the massive thighs, knees, and feet, ending in a thick fringe of

89

roots. Dragging the thrashing Keriags up by their legs, it grew to its full height, lifting them struggling off the ground with ease . . . and then, it raised them up and smashed them to the ground, where they lay crumpled and broken.

Behind her, only vaguely aware of what was going on, Hochi was stroking Elani's hair, shaking her gently. "Come on, girl. Come back. You just took a knock, that's all. You'll be okay." And indeed, the wound on her head was not as bad as it first appeared. It bled a lot, but that was the way of all head wounds, big or little. But it was not deep. Just a gash.

Of course, if she didn't regain consciousness soon, it wouldn't matter how deep it was. None of them would ever leave this plateau.

Hochi tilted his head up, looking out at the shadowy alleys between the buildings that crowded close. The Keriags were getting closer, fast. And this time, the single golem that stood in the Parakkans' defense would not be enough to stop them.

Above them, Ty pulled himself up the last of the rungs, clambering on to the roof of the Bear Claw. The entrance hatch was in front of him, an iron rectangle of riveted metal that provided access to the cockpit of the vehicle. All around him, the protrusions and lumps that crowded the Bear Claw's back confused the eye. He turned around and shouted down to the others: "Come on! Move it!" Waiting long enough to see that some of them, at least, had begun to ascend after him, he turned back to the hatch.

And saw Whist crouched there, three of his sharp-ended discs held between the fingers of his armoured glove, the omnipresent Blink by his side.

"You're not going nowhere without me," he snarled.

"Get out of the way," Ty said, his voice like grit.

"If you're getting off Os Dakar, I'm coming with you," Whist repeated, his painted face deadly serious, his gloved hand hovering, ready to throw its deadly pay-load.

"After what you've done? I doubt it."

"You know what it's like here. You play the hands you're sure of."

"So now you don't have Kettin to protect you any-more," Ty said, mock-sympathetic. "Really, I'd cry blood for you if I had time. But I don't. Get out of my way."

Blink growled, low in his throat.

Tochaa and Gerdi were halfway up the side of the Bear Claw when the second wave of Keriags arrived, breaking on the shabby buildings and washing down the narrow alleys towards them. Hochi was frantically patting Elani's face, urging her to wake up. Kia's eyes were closed in concentration, her attention focused on the golem that she animated. Ryushi stood next to her, as weaponless as she was, but with his stones boiling full of power. Once he let it go, he wouldn't be able to rein it in again. Not until he had drained himself dry. He would have one chance, and one chance only.

Would it be enough?

The Keriags fell on the golem like a swarm of locusts, presuming it to be the greatest threat. It was a terrifying sight, like razorfish converging on a wounded animal and stripping it to the bone. In seconds, the huge creature was roaring, subsumed under the tide of black, horny chitin, the Keriags easily evading its grasping hands with their superior speed. The shafts of their *gaer bolga* thrust in and out like the pistons of the magma derricks that loomed over Tusami City, stabbing and slashing, their backward-angled serrations tearing out chunks of the golem's earthy flesh as they were pulled free.

But the massacre of the golem only delayed the oncoming assault; for those Keriags that poured up behind the thrashing, bellowing mass merely swept around it, like a wave around a rock, and came skittering down towards the Bear Claw, their black eyes shining under their thick brows of jagged chitin.

Ryushi's fist clenched hard, the veins on the back of his hands standing out.

Then the Flow burst through him, sweeping along his veins like floodwater, blasting out of his outstretched hands to meet the attack, a vast, invisible pulse of concussion that swept forth in an arc. The air warped as the pulse drove it outward, a ripple, a wall of force that bulged around them and then smashed into the Keriags, blasting them apart, scattering them like dust, obliterating everything in its path. The nearest buildings collapsed, blown into rubble and splinters. The beleaguered golem was shattered, suffering the same fate as those who clung to it.

Somewhere, something huge roared, lifting its furious voice to the sky, a savage exultation in its freedom.

Ryushi became aware that he was yelling, the sound gradually sifting into his consciousness in the aftermath of the destruction. His cry died, leaving nothing but silence, a blasted world facing them in the twilight. For fifty feet in front of him, a patch of land had been cleared of everything, stripped clean. Beyond that, there were crumpled buildings, unidentifiable chunks of matter, things he would rather not think about.

93

But then the skittering started again. For the Keriags were endless, and more were on their way. And Ryushi had not a scrap left in him to protect them. He felt the exhaustion of draining his stones swoop upon him, felt Kia catch him and then stagger herself. She, too, was tired. Not like he was, but tired enough. The next Keriag attack would be the last thing they saw.

He looked back at Hochi. If it had not been for the fact that it was an unpardonable breach of manners to inquire about someone else's spirit-stones, he would have screamed: *Can't you* do *anything?* at the bigger man. How stupid, that here on the brink of the end he should care about the social niceties of the Dominions. But there it was; it was an irrevocable part of their lives that if a person chose not to reveal what their powers were they should respect that decision. Even unto death.

Behind them, in Hochi's arms, Elani stirred weakly.

Ty didn't know what the awesome burst of force was below them, but he felt the backlash of it across his shoulders. He was thrown forward into Whist, who was similarly surprised; but at the last moment he turned his fall into a dive, tackling his opponent to the bulkhead of the Bear Claw. The metal discs in Whist's hands flew free, rolling crazily away from them. Blink had fallen back, stunned by the eruption; now a flailing boot from Whist caught him on the side of his head, sending him sliding away on his side to thump into a steel heat-exhaust pipe with a whimper of pain.

The torchlight that had surrounded their position had been snuffed out by Ryushi's blast, and now Kia squinted into the unfamiliar pockets of darkness that sprawled among the rubble, trying to catch a sight of their enemy. The skittering of the Keriags had been drowned out now, pushed under by a low thunder that was getting louder, approaching, seeking the source of the destruction that had been felt right across the camp.

Three Keriags appeared, coming from their right, racing towards them suddenly. Kia twisted towards them, still holding her weakened twin. It would do no good. They had no defense. She could muster enough to delay them, maybe, but it would be a momentary grace.

Still, wasn't that one more moment worth trying for?

She never had time to answer her own question, because just then something massive lunged out of the darkness behind the Keriags, gathering them all in a single snap of its wide, fang-stuffed mouth and tossing them away. Kia's pupils dilated to pinpricks and her jaw fell open as she saw, at last, the creature that had been imprisoned in the Snapper Run. She did not know how it had gotten free. Maybe Kettin had released it, to cover his escape by sowing havoc, attacking friend and foe alike on its rampage.

It didn't matter, she thought, as it raised its head high and loosed a deafening bellow, a great sub-bass boom that rocked them all, these tiny figures that stood terrified in its presence. It didn't matter at all. It was here now, and that was the end of it.

It loomed over them, a massive, leathery thing with a humped back, standing on four huge legs that ended in three-toed claws. In the twilight, it was part of the shadow it had been born from, a huge silhouette against the Kirin Taq sun, of which the only distinct features were the two small, wide-set eyes and the vicious rows of long, narrow teeth, each as long as a man's arm.

Tochaa and Gerdi were paralyzed like the rest of them, near the top of the rungs on the side of the Bear Claw.

The monster's bellow faded, and in the silence that followed, it swung its blunted head to fix its cold gaze on them.

Ty had lashed a punch into Whist's face, and was drawing back for another one, when he heard the creature below. Like rabbits before a lion's roar, the two combatants looked up, frozen.

Only one of those present did not. Blink.

Ty saw him moving out of the corner of his eye, racing to save his master. He had recovered fast from his blow, scrambling to his feet and launching himself into a run, fangs bared, paws galloping over the roof of the Bear Claw towards Ty. The sight of the huge dog bearing down on him was enough to break Ty's paralysis, and he threw himself off Whist just as Blink gathered himself, bunching the muscles of his back legs to pounce. Ty scrambled away on his back, but he was too late to do anything about Blink's charge, and the dog pounced through the air at him, heading for his exposed throat. Frantically, moving on instinct, he drew his knees up into his body, the soles of his boots waiting to bear the brunt of the assault. He felt the breathtaking weight of the huge dog as his feet caught it just under the forelegs, and his knees were slammed back into his chest, bruising the muscle there; but then he shoved off, throwing the snarling mass of teeth and sinew away from him. At the same moment, Whist was getting to his feet, and Blink slammed into him, taking him off balance. He staggered backward, the dog entangled in his arms, and then pitched backward and over the edge of the Bear Claw with a cry, disappearing from sight.

Elani screamed in Hochi's arms.

Her eyes had flickered open at the sight of the awe-some creature that threatened them. They had focused, unfocused, fixed, and terror had swamped her, naked panic. She scrambled and thrashed in Hochi's arms, for she saw the beast rear at the sound of her shriek, shifting its attention to her, drawing back to bite at them.

Ryushi and Kia realized what was going to happen at the same moment. They threw themselves into Hochi, surrounding him and Elani with their arms, pushing them back against the cold body of the Bear Claw.

The monster lunged forward, teeth blurring in the twilight.

As one, they shut their eyes.

And the jaws snapped shut on nothing, nothing at all, and where there had been a huge machine, there was now an emptiness. The monster paused. For a moment, its tiny mind processed what had happened. Then it turned away, the massive bulk of its head swinging around and towards where the sounds of combat still raged.

There was much prey tonight.

3

More Than a Lifeline

From above, the forest was quiet, a vast, gently rippling blanket of yellow leaves that rested between the cradling arms of the mountains.

Under the skin of foliage, it was a different story.

Gar Jenna resounded to the clanks and thumps of action. Boots pounded the sturdy wooden platforms that jutted from the rock walls, hundreds of feet above the thin ribbon of river at the canyon floor. The walkways that were strung across the chasm were alive with traffic. Everywhere, people were moving, hauling loads or running to and fro. Pulleys whined as they operated lifts, shifting equipment and personnel between the many levels of the village, past the buildings and gantries that clung to the sheer sides of the chasm like limpets. Gar Jenna was mobilizing.

"The troops from Eran Tor have sent word," said the messenger, bowing low as he spoke. "They're ready and waiting."

"Good," Otomo said. The craggy face of the Keeper Elect of Gar Jenna was impassive beneath his grey-white hair, faded with the passing of fifty winters. He stood on the edge of the canyon, surrounded by the yellow-leaved nanka trees and yuki bushes that carpeted the forest-bowl, watching the activity beneath him. Overhead, the artificial leaf canopy that hid Gar Jenna from the air had been drawn across, and the thick ropes and pulleys that held it in place creaked gently in the slight wind.

The messenger looked at him expectantly, waiting to be dismissed, but Otomo suddenly asked: "How many wyverns can they muster?"

"The stables have produced four, perhaps five fighting wyverns," the messenger replied. The stables at Erin Tor had only recently been established, unlike Hochi's Stud in Tusami City or Banto's in the mountains. But, of course, the latter two had been seized by Macaan's troops; they had managed to salvage only a few wyverns from potentially dozens, and then only because the creatures had chanced to return to Parakka roosts elsewhere.

"How many does that make in all?" Otomo asked, his broad arms folded across his barrel chest. The messenger looked worried for a moment, and was preparing to politely tell the Keeper that he didn't know, he was just a messenger, when someone else spoke up from behind him.

"Thirty, or forty-five if Amanu Temple makes the muster. But we're short of riders."

Calica walked up to stand next to Otomo. She made a small bow with her head, her orange-gold hair slipping across her cheeks, and then turned to the messenger. "Thank you. Tell Erin Tor we are glad to have them with us, and to wait for the order to assemble."

The messenger bowed low and hurried away, into the surrounding trees. Calica's olive eyes followed Otomo's faded blue ones, watching the people of Gar Jenna swarming around many dozens of meters beneath them.

"They'll need a target," Otomo said.

"We don't have a target to give them," Calica replied.

"We have too *many* targets," he said.

"Which is exactly why we have to choose the right one," Calica answered. "You think we should try and take on Macaan's palace? I don't."

"We can't just wait to see what Macaan does, and then try to stop him. We're too small a force for defense," Otomo said, his voice deep and strong. "The only way we're going to win is if we attack."

"Attack *what*? The palace? Those huge termitary mounds? Maybe we could try and reclaim our posts in Tusami City?" Calica glanced sideways at him. "We'll only get one chance at this. We have to know we're going to do some good."

Otomo's massive shoulders lifted and settled in a sigh. "We should have tried harder. Even with our best spies, we couldn't get close enough. The Jachyra are too cursed good."

Calica was silent. She knew what had become of their people at the hands of Macaan's secret police. It wasn't something she preferred to think about.

"Have you any word on the betrayer?" Otomo said at length.

"We have no idea."

"So now we know little more than we did before," he concluded grimly. "Only that whatever is going to happen, it's going to happen soon."

"Unless, of course," Otomo's voice continued in Calica's other ear, "that particularly handsome green-haired kid and his friends come up with something in Os Dakar."

Otomo and Calica turned as one to see . . . *Otomo*, standing there with his arms crossed in an exact replica of the way he always stood. Otomo swore in surprise at seeing himself, and Calica's hand flew to her heart, a smile breaking on her face as she realized who it was.

"Gerdi, you *startled* me," she chided.

The other Otomo was gone, and in his place stood the young Noman boy, beaming a cheeky grin at them. "Sorry. Couldn't resist. How's tricks, anyway? What's all this about?" He motioned at the frantic activity below them in the canyon.

"Are you all alright?" Calica asked, her shock being replaced by relief and excitement that he had made it back from Os Dakar. "Did you get Ty? Is Ryushi okay?"

"Ryushi, eh?" Gerdi insinuated, giving her an exaggeratedly knowing wink.

"Shut *up*," she said, blushing despite herself. Otomo, next to her, tried to suppress a smile. "Are they okay?"

"All present and accounted for," he said. "Course, Elani's a little worse for wear, but then she *did* shift fifty-odd tons of metal as well as seven people across into the Dominions, so you gotta expect that."

"She did what?" Calica asked, not following.

Gerdi grinned. "We got Ty," he said. "And a couple of extra surprises, too. You wanna come see?"

Calica looked at Otomo, half to ask his permission — although she didn't really need it; they were of equal rank, even though she was only seventeen winters and he was three times her age — and half to see if he wanted to come.

"I'll expect a full report tonight at the longhouse," he said, his eyes kind.

"You'll get it," she said, then ruffled Gerdi's green hair. "I never thought I'd be this happy to *see* you," she announced to the younger boy.

"Touch my hair again and you'll lose that hand," Gerdi said, only half joking, and then led her off into the forest.

The walk to where the others were took a little less than an hour. On the way, Gerdi recounted to Calica everything that had happened since they had left for Os Dakar, suitably embellishing his own part in the proceedings. It was only fair. After all, since he'd gone to all the trouble of telling the story, he should be allowed to lionize himself a little. Calica repeatedly interrupted him to ask why they had sent Gerdi to come and find her instead of coming themselves, but Gerdi only sing-songed, "You'll see," and then cackled at the expression of pique on her face.

After a time, the forest petered out and turned into plains at the open end of the mountain range. Out in the clear, the sun of the Dominions was just reaching its zenith, and the faded green grass blew dry under its heat. Calica knew this area; nearby was a cave, where Parakka had often stockpiled supplies and weapons because moving them through the thick forest would be too troublesome. It was empty now; everything had been taken and was being hastily assembled for war.

"Hey!" She heard a shout from the tree line behind them, and she turned to see Ryushi rushing across the grass, a broad smile on his face. She raised her hand in greeting, but to her surprise he swept her up in his arms and hugged her, spinning her around in the air. She returned his hug uncertainly, and when they parted, she looked at him with an odd expression on her face.

"Feeling sprightly today?" she asked sarcastically.

"It's this sunshine," Ryushi replied, blinking up at the blinding orb in the sky. "Didn't realize how much I'd missed it, even for just a few days."

"How're things?" she asked.

105

"Getting better," he replied. "Kia's almost back to her old self again, since we got Ty. You?"

"Not so good," she admitted. "Macaan's massing his troops. Mostly around his palace, but also around all those weird mounds that I told you about —"

"Ley Warrens," Ryushi interjected.

"So you did find *some*thing out," Calica observed. "Anyway, we're gathering Parakkan forces in secret, but we're far outnumbered. We don't know what Macaan plans to do. We can only wait for him to make his move, and then try and stop him." She glanced at Gerdi, who was wearing a smug grin, and then back at Ryushi. "Unless you two have something to tell me . . . ?"

"It's more of a case of what *you* can tell *us*," Gerdi hinted cryptically.

"What's *that* supposed to mean?" she asked, exasperated.

"Come on," Ryushi offered. "I'll show you."

They walked back to where the others were waiting, just inside the edge of the forest, sheltering from the sun. They were sitting around a campfire, above which a small pot of rice and dried fish was simmering, delicious smells wafting from it. Greetings were made all around, and Calica was introduced to Ty. She had to admit, after Ryushi's description of him, she hadn't expected the fierce-looking tribal warrior that stood before her; but when he spoke, he was not half so intimidating as he first appeared and anyway, it took a lot to intimidate Calica. She exchanged nods of mutual respect with Tochaa; they had met before, during Parakka's attempts to set up a branch in Kirin Taq. Elani, who was sitting with her back against a tree, favored her with a weary smile; but Kia was strangely cold with her, and she saw Ryushi look surprised and disappointed at his sister's reaction. Calica did not share his surprise, however. Kia had been getting gradually more and more hostile towards her ever since they had met. What did Kia have against her, anyway?

"What happened to that Whist guy you were telling me about?" she asked Gerdi.

Gerdi scratched his ear and shrugged. "Everything that was touching the Bear Claw when Elani shifted us got brought over into the Dominions. He and his dog weren't. Ty says they went off the edge, but as to what happened to him . . . I dunno, I'm just glad he's gone."

"The Bear Claw? What?" Calica asked. "Is that the other surprise?"

"Later," Ryushi said. "Sis, you got that earring?"

"Like I'm going to *forget* it," Kia chided him, passing over the small band of silver, studded with minuscule diamonds. Her eyes flicked to Calica for an instant, and she seemed to freeze over a little; but the moment passed, and all was normal again.

"This," said Ryushi, "is King Macaan's own earring."

"Hopefully," Ty added, reminding them all that they had only Kettin's word it was genuine. But Calica didn't seem to hear; her attention was fixed entirely on the object held out in Ryushi's hand.

"Really?" she asked, her face transformed by wonder. "Is it really?"

Ryushi glanced sidelong at Ty. "Well, we were kinda hoping you could tell us."

"Give it to me," she said, and as Ryushi delivered it into her hand, she wore an expression of complete hope and fascination. If this was what he said it was, then this was more than a lifeline for Parakka; this could be the key to the whole of Macaan's plan.

The earring, dropped from Ryushi's hand, seemed to fall in slow motion towards her cupped palms, like a stone dropped in honey.

It touched her skin, and she was buried under the explosion of visions that hit her, smashing into her, sending her spinning into blackness. . . .

*　　　*　　　*

. . . and then she was *behind* his eyes, riding in the head of the young prince, but she couldn't see very much because of the tears that blurred everything and made the torchlight sparkle. What she did see was a deathbed, and on it two people, a man and a woman. Father and Mother. His father was a Kirin, his mother fair and blonde, a Dominion woman. But both of them had been ravaged by the terrible disease that had carried them off, and the boy was yet young, so young. He turned his head, and Calica traveled with him, to lay his eyes on a young Dominion girl, one of his mother's serving-maids, and Calica knew with a foresight that was not hers that he would marry this girl one day, and that she would bear him a daughter, and then be taken from him by the same disease that had laid his parents to rest. . .

. . . and now he was a King, the ruler of Kirin Taq, who had built on his father's legacy to subjugate all opposition against him. Calica watched as the last of the thanes of Kirin Taq knelt before him. And all around were the black-armoured forms of the King's Guardsmen, the troops that had been his father's and were now his. He turned away from the defeated thane, Calica traveling with him, and walked through the cool corridors of the palace towards his daughter's bedchamber. His wife was already dead by now, and Calica felt the pain as keenly as if it were her own. How strange, that a monster like this could love so deeply. But then he was leaning over his baby daughter, sleeping in her crib, and waving away the Guardsmen who watched over her. The door swung shut behind him with a heavy thump.

"All this for you," he said, and in those words Calica felt the deep adoration he had for his daughter, the only part of his wife he had left; and she knew, with a sharp twist of sorrow, that as his daughter grew she would not reciprocate that love, but be cold and cruel and beautiful. . . .

. . . and now Calica saw her, as a young woman, tall and slender and proud, with raven-black hair plaited in twists and falling over a simple blue gown. And she recognized those sculpted cheekbones, those ice-blue eyes, the perfect mouth twisted in a triumphant smile. Aurin. The Princess Aurin, ruler of Kirin Taq; for that was what she was now. But there was something curious in the sight, something fundamentally disturbing, because her recognition of the Princess was not just through the King's eyes, but through her own as well. For though she had never physically laid eyes on Aurin, there was . . . *something* . . .

. . . and now Calica felt Macaan's pride as he left his daughter to rule over the subjugated land, while he massed his army around him and made ready to leave for new territories. For his desire to conquer was insatiable; she felt Macaan's thoughts writhing in his brain, telling him that his days were numbered, that one day the disease that had taken his parents and lover away from him would be back, and this time it would be *him* it claimed. The King was working against time, trying to obtain the world for his daughter and knowing, deep down, that even that would not be enough to wring love from her heart. . . .

. . . and now Macaan is King of the Dominions, too. His army of Guardsmen have taken the old King by surprise, appearing on the battlefield as if from nowhere and annihilating the pitiful inland defense, cutting off supplies to the coast and then sweeping out to finish the job. Because Macaan has a machine, a machine powered by Resonants, with a strength so great that it can shift whole armies across the time-gap between Kirin Taq and the Dominions. But there is a problem; it can be used only once, for the Resonants are frail things and don't survive the transition. That one time is enough to crush King Oko and his Knights, and take over the Dominions. But it is not enough to fulfil him. Even now, he isn't satisfied with what he has; because he lacks the forces to achieve complete control, and only complete control will secure his daughter's reign. So he turns his mind to the plan. . . .

"*Oh!*" Calica yelped, dropping the earring as if it had burned her. For a moment, she looked like a frightened animal, paralyzed by a predator; but then her eyes calmed a little, and she looked around at the faces that peered at her in concern.

"Are you okay?" Ryushi asked. "You can't have held it for more than a second."

"The plan! The *plan!*" Calica cried, springing to her feet. "I know what he's going to do!"

Broken Sky

Act One
Part Nine

Broken Sky

1

Dry and Blackened

"Macaan? What —" Tochaa began, but Calica steam-rollered him, desperate and urgent, reeling at the enormity of what she had seen.

"The Ley Warrens, the way he's been gathering Resonants, the massing of armies . . . it all fits now! It was just so *big*, none of us could see it!"

"What *is* it? What's he going to do?" Hochi demanded.

Calica paced the grass restlessly, agitated. "We found out from Ty that he was taking the Resonants that he captured to the Ley Warrens, right? Gerdi told me that much. But listen . . . the Ley Warrens are nothing more than huge power amplifiers. They're positioned across the Dominions along the ley lines — the bands of energy under the earth where the Flow is strongest. It's like he's making a . . . a *net*, to cover the whole land, a net of boosting points for the Flow. And he's been taking Resonants to the Ley Warrens because it's *them* who'll be providing the power."

"But Resonants can't do anything!" Elani protested, roused from her weariness. "All we can do is cross from Tweentime to here and . . . back . . ." She trailed off, her dark eyes widening in amazement. "Can he *do* that?" she breathed.

"Do *what*?" Hochi cried.

"He's going to integrate the worlds," Calica said, her voice silencing them all. "He's going to unify the Dominions and Kirin Taq." She paused. "And then he's going to invade us. He did a similar thing before, on a smaller scale, when he took the throne. He brought over an army, but the machine failed and he couldn't get reinforcements. This time he's going to do it properly."

"Invade us? The whole of the Dominions? With what? He doesn't have the manpower!" Hochi protested.

"*She* does," Tochaa said levelly. "His daughter. The Princess Aurin. And it's not *men*, either."

"Keriags?" Kia asked.

"Keriags," Tochaa agreed. "It'll be just like what happened at Os Dakar, but all over the Dominions. The

Princess has hundreds of thousands of Keriags at her command."

"But why invade us?" Gerdi said. "He's already the big cheese of the place. What's he got to gain?"

"Security," Calica replied, rubbing her eyes with her knuckles to try and knead the lingering disorientation away. "Kirin Taq has already been put down. Tochaa, what kind of resistance do you have over there?"

"Not much," he admitted, his grey-skinned face impassive. "Isolated bands, mainly in the Rifts. Nothing like Parakka."

"Exactly!" Calica replied, suddenly excited. "Nothing like Parakka. Parakka couldn't have formed in Kirin Taq. There are more troops there, closer control. Here, he's tried to suppress any bad word against him, he's tried to cover up what he's done so people won't know, he's got everyone afraid to speak out in case the Jachyra might hear them . . . but that's all to keep our eyes off the main issue. And that is that Macaan does not have a strong foothold here! And he *knows* that the more he tightens his grip, the more people will join Parakka and in time, in *time* . . . we can beat him."

"Unless he crushes us now," Ryushi finished morosely, then ran his hand through his quills and muttered, "Great."

Calica spoke again in the long silence that followed. "The Ley Warrens are bridges. When they all operate together, they will exist in both worlds at once. They will become passing-places, where an ordinary, non-Resonant person can cross from Kirin Taq to the Dominions and back again, freely. When that happens, the Keriags that he has massed inside those Warrens will pour out and swamp the Dominions. Parakka — or any kind of rebellion at all — will be overwhelmed. And the Dominions will be his. He calls it the Integration."

"But who are the Keriags? Why do they obey the Princess?" Gerdi asked, directing his question half to Tochaa and half to Calica.

"We don't know," Tochaa said, and Calica bowed her head, indicating that she, too, had no answer for him. "She has some kind of hold over them, but we have never been able to get close enough to find out."

The discussion faltered. The luscious smells of the rice and fish in the pot, the warm summer air, the hot sunlight that blazed just on the edge of their shelter of shade . . . they all seemed a mockery now. They were standing on the brink of the end of their way of life, the end of freedom, for them and everyone in the Dominions.

"So what happens now?" Gerdi asked.

"We fight," Kia said. "What else?"

"She's right," Calica said. "We may be able to stop this. If just one of the Ley Warrens is destroyed, if we can stop it operating, the whole network might be put out of commission. The ley lines that they run along feed power to the others, connect them all up. We might be able to take one of them out and wreck the whole thing, at least temporarily. That way we'll gain some breathing space, work out what to do next."

"That's a lot of *mights*," Kia said scornfully.

"Well, unfortunately we're at a little bit of a disadvantage here, as you may have noticed," Calica replied, heavily sarcastic, "and we have to go on what we've got."

"How are we gonna destroy it?" Ryushi asked, casting a sideways glance at his sister.

Calica looked at him, seeming to see past him, her eyes on something else. The avalanche of knowledge and sensation triggered by touching Macaan's earring – the earring he had worn most of his life, evidently, until he had lost it to Kettin — was still boiling in her head. She closed her eyes, trying to sift the relevant answer for him.

"The Resonants that he's been kidnapping, they provide the power. The Warren amplifies it. We have to find the Resonants inside the Warren, and free them somehow. Or stop them."

"*Kill* them?" Elani cried.

"If we have to," Kia answered in Calica's place. Ty looked at her, shocked. She returned his gaze levelly.

"If we have to," Calica echoed, her head bowing. "There may be no other way to avert the Integration. It would be their lives for many." Then suddenly she looked up, from Ryushi to Kia and back again, struck by a thought. "You two grew up on a wyvern Stud, didn't you? Can you fly?"

"Some," Ryushi admitted. "Not well. Why, you need flyers?" His voice had become excited at the thought of flying a wyvern again, and all his old passion for the creatures reignited inside him at the prospect. Oh, to be Bonded, to share a link like that with a wyvern . . . He fingered the Bonding-stone at his throat, a gift from his father. That was his dream, a dream that he had been forced to forget in the surge of tragedies that had befallen him. But if he couldn't be Bonded, he could at least *fly*.

"We need everyone," Calica said. "If we're going to try and take out one of those Warrens, we can expect heavy resistance."

"I'm going as well," Elani said. Everyone looked at her.

"El, you can't," Ryushi said. "You can't fight."

"I don't mean *fight*," she said, and her voice was once more that of a much older girl, one who had borne a lifetime's worth of sorrow and experience in a few short and hard years. "No one knows what those places are like inside. You need me to guide you. Wherever the Resonants are, I can find them. You know how Macaan's men could always tell when and where we crossed over? It's the same for all of us; we can sense when one of ours tries to shift. If they're using their power, I can take you to them." She glared at them defiantly. "Don't say you don't need me."

"Elani, you're not the only Resonant in Parakka. . . ." Calica said, but she didn't sound like her whole heart was in the argument.

"But I'm the *best* one and you know it!" she pouted. "Cousin Ryushi'll protect me."

Ryushi nodded. The promise he had made to his father a long time ago, to protect this girl with his life, was one of the few surviving pieces of their past. Just as Kia clung to Ty for her salvation, so he upheld his promise.

Calica looked away. She wasn't making any decisions now. She would have to take all this back to the Council at Gar Jenna, and they would decide what was to be done. Her eyes fell to where Macaan's earring lay on the ground. Following her gaze, Ryushi picked it up and pocketed it.

"Gerdi," she said. "You mentioned something called the Bear Claw. You also said something about Elani shifting fifty tons of metal. I assume the two are connected?"

Gerdi grinned. "You remember that old storage cave near here, that we used to use all the time? Come and have a look. We brought back a little bonus from Os Dakar. Something that just might give us the edge we need. You wanted to know why we dragged you all the way out here? This is why."

They left the shade to follow where Gerdi led them. They moved as if in a dream, reeling from the terrible news that they had received, all except Kia dreading the conflict to come. And soon, they were gone, leaving the fire to burn itself out in the heat of the midday sun.

Unnoticed, the pot of rice and fish boiled dry and blackened.

2

Together in a Tide

South of Tusami City, the veldt stretched as far as the eye could see. Yellowed, sun-beaten grass rippled lazily with the hot breeze. Clusters of pagoda trees, with their strange, disc-shaped leaves, dotted the landscape here and there, interspersed occasionally with the lonely, knotted shape of a kinyan or the thorny barbs of a jujip bush. Dusty trails meandered across the vast plains, well-traveled routes between the great mountain city to the north and the settlements to the south and west. Only a single land-train plied the trails today, the rising yellow cloud of its slow passage feathering and drifting away behind it. Distantly, a herd of banaki — huge, shaggy, slow-moving beasts — cropped the dry grass or lowed their distinctive rumble.

Standing alone, rising out of the earth like a long-fingered hand, the Ley Warren split the clear blue sky.

It was comprised of five enormous towers of earth, the deep reddish-brown earth of the veldt, packed tight and baked hard as stone. They jutted accusingly towards the sun overhead, gnarled and crooked and uneven, of different heights and widths but all breathtaking in their sheer scale. At their bases, they were joined together in one huge mass, and bridging the gaps between them at seemingly random intervals were spidery tunnels and narrow walkways, strung impossibly through the air without any kind of structural support.

Yet even though the construction bore no signs of human hands in its making, the King's troops were in evidence all around. Force-cannon turrets studded every surface, with the green carapace of the Artillerists evident at each one. Guardsmen stood silent at watch, their black armour glinting in the sun. Ramps and tunnels crisscrossed the exterior, along which Crawlers and cricktracks moved slowly, hauling loads into and out of the Warren through the many entrances that pocked its base. The whole huge construction shimmered as if in a heat-haze, though it was not the heat but the raw *power* stockpiled inside that bent the air around it.

The horizon was clear.

Almost.

For a keen-eyed Guardsman, standing atop a tributary parapet of one of the highest towers, had focused his attention on something in the east. Something . . . odd. The tiniest, most imperceptible blur in the distance. Behind the glare-resistant eyepieces of his visor, his pupils were fixed on it. Slowly, with a mounting suspicion, he drew up the long, brass barrel of a telescope, careful not to point it at the sun, which would blind him even through his visor. And he looked. And he saw.

And then he turned, and ran down the narrow, winding steps, to raise the alarm within.

"Ya-*haaa*!" Ryushi whooped in exultation as he banked his wyvern to swoop over the huge, rumbling mass that was the Bear Claw. Beneath him, the entire assembled forces of Parakka were advancing across the veldt, five thousand strong or more. Anything and everything that could have been employed for warfare had been brought. Cricktracks rattled alongside horses and the occasional pakpak from Kirin Taq. From the southern deserts, there were *mukhili* — enormous armoured beetles that were like living tanks — which lumbered through the milling masses under the control of their handler's spirit-stones, each one carrying fifty or more desert-folk in howdahs. From the West, the heart of the Machinist's Guild, there were war engines of dulled and weathered iron and steel that steamed and roared as they ground their way across the plains. And everywhere there were Parakkans, people from all corners of the Dominions, united in their hatred of Macaan's oppressive regime. Swords glittered, the air hummed with the power of engorged spirit-stones, and the noise, the deafening, all-encompassing noise of war . . . it swept them all up, carried them along with it, joining them together in a tide of adrenaline and the anticipation of battle.

Behind Ryushi in the harness rode Elani and Calica. The little girl clung tightly to Ryushi's belt, her cheek buried in his back. Half of her was wishing that she had never insisted on coming, that she could be back at Gar Jenna now in safety; but the other half, the one that had learned its lessons through hard and bitter experience, fortified her and told her that what she did was necessary. If King Macaan prevailed, not even Gar Jenna would be safe.

Calica's orange-gold hair flew out behind her, whipping and writhing in the wind of the wyvern's flight. She looked across the sky to either side of her. Forty wyverns, all told. Amanu Temple had joined the struggle at the eleventh hour, providing them with fifteen more of the beasts, but five had been left at Gar Jenna because there was nobody who could ride them. Of those forty that flew, twenty-seven had been kitted out with force-cannons, operated by defected Artillerists or those who had the relevant spirit-stones to use them but had managed to avoid being "recruited" by Macaan.

Forty wyverns. It was not many. But it would have to do.

She glanced over at Kia, who was riding a wyvern to their right with Gerdi, and then over at Hochi on their other side. He was an expert wyvern-rider, having been the master of a Stud in Tusami City for a good many years. Tochaa rode with him; it was a development Hochi seemed frankly a little unhappy about, although he had not complained. The mistrust of Kirins was a common and widespread thing, even among Parakkans, but Calica had decided to put their Kirin ally with someone he knew rather than a stranger.

Hochi nodded slowly to Calica, his hands gripped ready on the nerve-points to either side of the wyvern's great neck.

Calica raised her arm. All the riders' eyes turned to her. And then she dropped it, and forty pairs of hands dug into the nerve-points on their wyverns, sending the

127

creatures surging forward with a great triumphant screech, leaving the rumbling mass of the ground forces to diminish behind them. The wyverns' great armoured rear wings scythed the air, their smaller, frontmost set tilting up and down to manipulate the airflow and steer them. The veldt sped by beneath, a blurred carpet of green-yellow with only the occasional group of pagoda trees whooshing past to break the uniformity. But up ahead, the Ley Warren loomed, its tall spires of earth gradually ascending out of the horizon.

Calica ran over the plan of attack in her head, searching it again and again for weaknesses as she had done all night. The truth was, though, that it was so simple and straightforward that weaknesses were not really a factor. They had no idea what the Ley Warren was like inside; all they could do was hope to breach the outer defenses, and then try and cope with what was within. This was a straightforward assault, a last-ditch attempt, relying not on subtlety or strategy but on what little brute force Parakka could muster.

The wyverns were to form the vanguard of the army. Those with force-cannons were to try and take out the Warren's defenses and cover the other wyverns, who were going to attempt to get close enough to penetrate the main structure and find whatever mechanism or device was at its core. Meanwhile, the ground forces headed by Ty and the Bear Claw would arrive, hopefully finding the outer defenses destroyed. This would allow them to engage whatever ground troops the Warren might employ.

That was the plan. And it was all that stood between King Macaan and complete control of the Dominions.

"You ready, Ryushi?" Calica cried against the howling wind in her face.

Ryushi looked back at her with a fierce grin. The excitement of flying a wyvern again warred with the nervousness in his belly and bubbled and fizzed inside him. "Ready as I'll ever be."

Calica nodded, swallowing against her own fear. She could maintain a façade of strength, but she couldn't fool herself. She was terrified. Beneath the desperate rush of battle that charged them, they were *all* terrified.

Then the force-cannons opened up.

The first bolt from the Warren split the air not far from Kia's head, lashing her dark red ponytail with the force of its passage. She cried out and banked away, and the others, seeing her, broke the loose formation they had been following and scattered, swooping and climbing and swerving as the first bolt was succeeded by a second, and a third. Deadly, near-invisible ripples of en-

129

ergy lanced out from the Warren, making up in frequency what they lacked in accuracy. The riders evaded them as best they could, speeding towards their target, attempting to get close enough to return fire.

Ryushi squeezed his eyes shut as a wyvern close below him took a direct hit. There was a sickening *whump*, and then it fell behind them, flailing broken-winged towards the ground, its rider already dead on its back.

This is real, he thought. *Oh, Father, protect me now.*

The air pulsed around them, warping in the wake of the bolts of concussion that fired from the Warren, but Kia did not fear them. Fear had become nothing to her now. Only hate fired her, the hatred of Macaan and all his representatives. The hatred of the one who was responsible for her family's death. She had reclaimed Ty, but she could never reclaim them. And while the raw wounds of her grief had begun to close in the arms of the Pilot, her thirst for revenge had not been quenched. Not yet. Maybe not ever.

But now they were close enough to the Warren so that it filled their view, and she could see the rotating gun-platforms that nestled on parapets and in the banks of earth, hissing steam as they swiveled to rotate the fifteen-foot-long cannons, tracking their targets. She could see, too, the blank visors of dark green, the glassy eyepieces of the Artillerists. And she hated.

"What are you *doing*?" Gerdi howled, as she threw the wyvern forward and swooped in towards the Warren. "Let our guys take out the cannons first!"

But Kia didn't reply. Her jaw was set, her eyes hard. She wanted to hurt them, as they had hurt her, and nothing was going to stop her.

"Kia!" Ryushi cried from the other wyvern, seeing her surge ahead; but the air suddenly erupted all around him as the Parakkan troops opened up with their own force-cannons, smashing into the Warren and blasting clouds of earth from its vast flanks. A bolt screamed into one of the gun emplacements with deadly force, blasting it inward and leaving only a twisted, smoking crush of metal in its place. Ryushi dived hard to avoid a blast from a cannon near the base of the Warren, and then came up turning, angling himself to intercept his sister.

"Where are you going?" Calica cried to Ryushi. In between them, Elani had become very small and quiet, her eyes shut tight as her black hair whipped and flailed around her cheeks.

"I'm going with her!" he shouted back, and a moment later he ducked instinctively as another wyvern swooped over his head, its black underbelly sliding through the sky above them. It was Hochi and Tochaa; they, too, were following Kia on her breakaway course. Ryushi dug in his fingers and spurred his wyvern to accompany them.

Across the plains, the advancing Parakkan army drew ever closer.

Inside the cockpit of the Bear Claw, Ty sat hunched forward in concentration. It took all of his skill to power the huge machine, to force life into its Machinist heart and make its cogs grind, its pistons pump, its gears mesh. He was sweating, droplets of moisture tracking from his bald scalp over his particolored face. His knuckles stood out as he clenched the handgrips that steered the beast, keeping it straight.

Next to him sat Otomo, his arms crossed. He was looking through the narrow gash that afforded the driver a view of the outside world. Through the smoky dimness of the cockpit, the sunlight blazed painfully bright, making sparkling motes and swirls in the air before his eyes. The roar of the Bear Claw surrounded him; the iron fixtures rattled as the vehicle rumbled towards the Warren.

He narrowed his eyes against the glare. The Ley Warren was a war zone now, force-bolts flying in all directions as the Parakkan wyverns circled and swooped like moths around a glowstone. He could hear nothing at this distance, and certainly not over the bellowing engine of the Bear Claw, but he watched the battle being played out silently, and he prayed for all their sakes that they would be victorious.

"Not so *close*!" Gerdi bleated as Kia sent them into a dive underneath one of the earthen walkways that spanned the gap between two of the towers. She didn't hear him. Her attention was fixed on the gun that spat at them from beneath a protective overhang. She could see three Artillerists manipulating it, turning it on its steam-driven tracks, angling it upwards towards them.

A cold smile flickered over her face, and her spirit-stones blazed.

The overhang collapsed, slumping down on the Artillerists and burying them under a ton of hardened earth before they had time to realize what had happened. She swept away from them, leaving a slowly dispersing haze of dust in her wake, and two wyverns followed her, those of Ryushi and Hochi.

"There doesn't seem to be any air defense other than these cannons!" Ryushi yelled, the wind carrying his voice back to Calica. "No wyverns!"

She brushed a lashing strand of hair out of her eyes

and nodded, unseen, at his observation. As they had suspected, Macaan's resources were spread thin, and there were too many Ley Warrens to protect them all adequately. His forces were concentrated around his palace. There were no wyverns to engage them here; and if they were lucky, no way they could get there in time to stop them. It was a frail sliver of hope, but it was better than nothing.

"Sis! Get us inside!" Ryushi shouted, but it was hopeless. Kia wasn't hearing him. But Gerdi, who was looking back over his shoulder, saw Ryushi's motions and guessed what he meant.

"Hey, Kia!" he said. "Remember why you're here! We've got to get inside the Warren!"

Kia gritted her teeth, and a strip of earth detonated beneath her, destroying another gun emplacement. The concentration of fire was beginning to lessen now, as the Parakkan fighters were finding their targets; but it was still frantic, and they were forced to dodge and weave manically, pushing the screeching wyverns to their limits.

"Kia! Hey, listen!" Gerdi shouted, shaking her shoulder. But she would not hear him. Her eyes were already searching out the next target, scanning the vast earthen walls that loomed around them. She spied a gun atop a high parapet, and with a nod she sent it toppling, the huge metal weapon falling past them, accompanied by shrieking Artillerists. Again, and again, the gun emplacements fell beneath her fury, crushed by the earth that protected them or sent falling as their foundations collapsed. Kia was a wave of destruction, sweeping between the towers and leaving devastation in her wake, possessed by icy fury. It was all Ryushi and Hochi could do to keep up with her.

Singlehandedly, she was giving Parakka the edge. The other wyverns were rallying to her, given heart by her strength, swooping and wheeling around her to destroy those emplacements that she missed. Heedless of her own safety, she threw herself at the enemy, boiling with the need for revenge; and the Parakkan troops responded, attacking the Warren with redoubled vigor. But the cost to herself was mounting. Gerdi felt her ribs trembling under his hands, her breathing become labored, but still she would not stop.

"Sis!" Ryushi shouted again, and once more went unheard. She was letting her hate get in the way of the plan; for though her reckless assault was winning the battle against the Warren's defenses, she was the one who had to create the opening to let the other riders into the Ley Warren. The walls were too thick for force-cannons.

And then a voice cut through the fog of Kia's freezing

rage. A deep, reassuring voice, one that brought her up short and made tears start to her eyes.

It was Banto. Her father's voice. Coming from over her shoulder.

"Kia, daughter, remember why you are here. I created Parakka to defeat Macaan, not to slake your thirst for vengeance. Don't let my work be in vain."

"Gerdi," she said, through gritted teeth. "I am gonna *kill* you for that."

And then she swept out an arm, and a wide section of one of the towers exploded outward beneath them, geysering out rocks and chunks of dirt as big as a man. The wall was breached; the troops had a way in.

"Go! Go! *Go!*" shouted Calica, and both Ryushi and Hochi peeled their wyverns away simultaneously, arrowing towards the ragged hole in the earthen fortifications of the Ley Warren. Those wyverns that did not have force-cannons followed their lead, and though Calica noted that their numbers were heavily diminished, they cried out in triumph as they poured towards the breach.

But when Ryushi looked back, he saw that Kia wasn't coming with them. She stayed to destroy the remainder of the outer defenses, and the other riders flocked to her like a beacon.

*   *   *

That was when the Keriags attacked.

They boiled out of the Warren like black blood out of a picked scab, their high-kneed legs ratcheting, carrying their low-slung torsos along. From everywhere they came, out of the hundreds of tunnels that honeycombed the interior, scuttling down ramps, or simply squeezing through tiny holes in the walls and skittering down the near-vertical sides. And with them came the Guardsmen and their vehicles, circling around the perimeter of the Warren on either side in a pincer motion, aiming to catch the Parakkan troops in the flanks.

"We've stirred them up now!" Otomo said, a taut smile twisting his stern face, illuminated in the bright slash of light that beamed through the viewing-port of the Bear Claw.

Ty didn't reply, his entire concentration set on handling the metal creature he commanded. His stones burned in his back as he fought to sustain power to its mechanisms.

The armies came together at almost exactly the same moment. The Keriags swept into the front ranks, the dazzling sun running along the vicious barbs of their *gaer bolga*. They darted and slashed and stabbed into the fray, and battle was joined. Simultaneously, the Guardsmen and their Crawlers and cricktracks hit the flanks of the Parakkan army; but not with their full force. As Otomo had expected, they were mainly hanging back, protecting the entrances to the Warren and preventing the Parakkans from getting inside. It was a sound strategy, but it also halved their potential for damaging the attackers. Otomo leaned forward and looked up through the viewing-port at where the wyverns still wheeled overhead, trading force-cannon shots. The ground troops would buy them time to get inside. He had to hope that they would come through.

Blades slashed and blood flew, and the air shrieked with the discharge of spirit-stones. A rider howled as a Keriag took him full in the chest with one of their deadly barbed spears, and its companions fell on him like wolves as he hit the ground, the hafts of their *gaer bolga* thrusting up and down. Elsewhere, their chitinous bodies cracked and splintered as they were ground under the caterpillar tracks of a Parakkan war-machine. Force-bolts stabbed in and out of the fray, smashing those they hit like a hammer on an egg. One of the mukhili, its broad back swarming with desert-folk, was lumbering around amid the churning mass of figures, sweeping up Keriags in its mandibles and crushing them. The hum of defensive shields was a constant undertone to the peaks and troughs of noise, the swell of battle, the clash of weapons, and the yells and screams of men and women as they fought, and killed, and died.

But Otomo was concerned, in the noisy haven of the Bear Claw's cockpit. The Keriags were too many, and too vicious. They were steadily wearing down the Parakkans, taking them apart bit by bit. This was exactly what Calica had feared; in a stand-up fight, Parakka simply did not have the numbers to overcome even a poorly defended structure like a Ley Warren. It would have to be either all-out attack, or they would have to find a more defensible place to fight. Either way, that meant that they had to get out of the open. And to do that, they would have to get inside the Warren.

His eyes scanned the entrances as the Bear Claw juddered, crunching a group of Keriags that were too tightly packed to evade it underneath its tracks. No dice there; they were too well-defended, and had been constructed to be particularly difficult for attackers to gain them.

So they would have to make their own entrance.

"There's no way in," Otomo said calmly, his eyes ranging the huge wall of reddish earth that soared above them. "Do you think we can break through?"

Ty glanced at him, sparing him a moment of his attention from the demands of the vehicle. "It'll hurt," he said.

"Your call," Otomo replied.

There was a pause.

"Guess I owe somebody for all that blood on my hands, huh?" Ty said.

Otomo didn't reply.

"Hold on," Ty said. "Let's make this heap of junk worth something."

The Bear Claw's engine bellowed deafeningly, and it began to pick up speed, pulling away from the mass of the battle, its exhaust pipes belching scalding steam. Ty's teeth were gritted in the dimness of the cockpit; his veins stood out stark against the muscles of his forearms and in his neck. His whole body shook, pouring every ounce of his being into the vehicle around him, goading the awesome beast into a charge. Gradually, the distance between the Bear Claw and the main mass of ground forces increased, like a slow-motion arrow shot from a bow, and it picked up velocity as it steamed and roared towards the blank face of the Ley Warren's wall. Force-bolts hammered the outer skin of the vehicle, rocking it but not slowing it down. Kia and the wyvern-riders had done their job well, for only a few emplacements remained to threaten them, and it would take more than that to stop the Bear Claw.

Closer came the wall. Closer, until it seemed to fill the whole world outside their hazy, dark cockpit.

Otomo braced himself.

Collision.

Ty and Otomo were thrown forward, slammed bodily against the iron of the cockpit as the Bear Claw shuddered with the terrific impact. There was an instant of bright pain, so bright that it stole Ty's breath; and then the pain was gone, and blackness took him.

But the Bear Claw kept going, propelled by its own momentum. With an awesome crash, it ploughed into the wall of the Ley Warren, breaking the mass of baked earth that was the outer skin. Huge boulders of the red-brown dirt of the veldt crumbled around the vehicle as it smashed inward, an immense metal battering ram.

And then, after the tumult . . . silence. The Bear Claw halted, buried inside the Warren. The last piece of rubble fell. A great tear gaped in the side of the Keriags' great fortress.

A great cheer went up from the assembled Parakkan forces. Force-cannons jabbed at them, spearing bolts of concussion into their ranks, but they made eagerly for the Warren, fighting with newly restored vigor, seeing a way in opened for them. The Keriags tried to organize to stop them, but they were swept under the tide and forced aside, and the Parakkan forces poured into the open wound, around the steaming, silent hulk of the Bear Claw, and began to clot and scab, some of them forming a line of defense across the gap while others surged into the veins and arteries of the Warren, sowing discord.

The Parakkan forces were in.

3

The Same Blood

Ryushi hacked and swung and parried, sweat flying from his face. The clear blood of the Keriags splashed his body as Calica struck home with her katana next to him. In the close press of the tunnels, high in the sky above the veldt, the fighting was hectic and desperate. Dark shapes lunged out of the gloom, lashing at them with their cruel spears. But the Keriags were gradually falling back, and the Parakkans, through sheer force of will, were driving them off.

The breach that Kia had opened for them had provided a place for them to land their wyverns; but there they had to dismount, for the tunnels and passageways of the Ley Warren's towers were too small to allow the creatures inside. They had forged inward, but had not traveled far before the first of the Keriags had attacked them. Since then, they had been harried every step of the way. Still, the resistance had been less than Ryushi had expected, and for that he was thankful. He suspected the bulk of the Warren's forces were defending on the ground.

The tunnels were surprisingly smooth-walled, with occasional glowstones embedded in the walls, floor, or ceiling providing a feeble orange light. They were high enough to walk along, wide enough for three abreast, and they branched off at random and crazy angles. It had been built by the Keriags to accommodate Guardsmen as well as their kind, but only just. The air was hot, dry, and stifling; some of the tunnels were so steep it was impossible to climb down them, and there was no decoration or amenities that they could see.

But none of this mattered to them. All that mattered was their mission.

"This way! Down here!" Elani cried, tugging at Ryushi's arm as the last of the latest wave of Keriags fell under Hochi's hammer.

Ryushi stepped over the fallen body of one of his comrades and crouched down next to her. "You sure, El?"

"It's starting," she said. "The power's building up, Cousin Ryushi. I can feel it."

Ryushi cursed under his breath and checked over his shoulder to be sure everyone was with him. "Okay, this way!" he shouted back to them, then put a hand on Elani's shoulder to move her protectively behind him.

They headed along a tributary tunnel that sloped downwards at a shallow angle. Ryushi, Hochi, and Tochaa took the lead, with Calica behind them. The big man kept on casting sidelong glances towards his Kirin companion, as if he was wary of letting him out of sight. Ryushi frowned momentarily; even after all they'd been through, Hochi still couldn't bring himself to trust a Kirin. What was so hard about it? There were people of all skin tones and cultures across the Dominions; why were the Kirins any different to them? In fact, now that he thought of it, he had noticed many of the other Parakkan fighters acting in much the same way. They tolerated Tochaa, but were ill at ease in his company.

He looked across at Tochaa, and the Kirin's light-colored eyes met his. He wondered how much of what he was thinking was apparent to the taller man.

They forged onward, their eyes and ears alert for any signs of a new attack. There were perhaps thirty of them — it was hard to tell in the bad light — and most of them were people whom Ryushi had never met, members of distant branches of Parakka. But at this moment, they were like brothers and sisters, united in danger and in a common belief, risking their lives for their cause.

Except Tochaa, of course. He was no one's brother here.

They came to a junction, where several large tunnels intersected at the same point, forming a wide cave. One narrow tunnel went vertically straight up, another angled off downward in a steep decline, while three others — including the one they were traveling down — crossed paths at this point. Even with the light of the glowstones that some of the Parakkans carried adding to those that were set in the walls, they could see little more than a few orange-hued meters down any of them.

"Where do we go?" somebody asked in a gruff, phlegmy voice.

That was when the Keriags sprang their ambush.

They had been lurking there, hiding on the edge of the light, only the faint sheen of their black eyes to show them up against the thick shadows. Ryushi had noticed the lack of real opposition since they had entered the Warren; now he had his reason why. The Keriags had been waiting for them, drawing them deeper into the Warren where there was no chance of escape; and now they struck.

They sallied out of the darkness, the cave filling with

the echoes of their feet clicking on the hard earth, and a cry of alarm went up from Calica. They came from all sides, pouring from the tunnels. In moments, the cave was a swarming mass of black bodies, and the Parakkans were surrounded.

For a heartbeat, there was silence, the troops facing each other in stillness, the hard eyes of the humans locked with the black, narrow orbs of the Keriags.

Then Hochi roared a battle cry, and the carnage began.

The two sides clashed in a frenzy. The Parakkan side comprised some of the best fighters in the Dominions, but the Keriags were fast and held superior numbers. Tochaa's twin knives slashed and parried, fighting alongside Hochi's great crushing hammer. Calica's katana cut a swath through the enemy, her catlike features twisted in a snarl of exertion. Ryushi stayed defensive, occasionally glancing back to be sure Elani was just behind him, within their circle of protection. Her eyes flashed and glittered in the faint light, wide with terror.

The cave was lit up by the flare of someone's spirit-stones, a short bolt of fire that blasted into the dark mass of Keriags. But few people in the Dominions had spirit-stones that could be used offensively, for most of them had been taken to join Macaan's Guardsmen; and fewer still possessed the kind of power that Ryushi did. The occasional jab of energy scored through the Keriags, but there were always others to scurry over the smoking husks of their brethren.

Ryushi longed to help, to release the pent-up energy inside him, but he didn't dare. If he drained himself again, who would protect Elani? No, he had made a promise, he —

"Ryushi! Get out of the *way*!"

He was moving before Calica's shouted warning had fully registered in his head, throwing himself sideways, his arm reaching to shove Elani aside as he did so. From above, a black shape dropped down from the earthen ceiling, and he barely had time to realize that the Keriags were crawling through the vertical tunnel overhead before he had to roll aside to avoid the downward thrust of a barbed spear. There was no second strike; Calica's blade carved into the creature, throwing it aside. But more of them were dropping down now, a lethal rain, detaching themselves from the ceiling and falling onto the heads of the Parakkans, stabbing and thrusting with their spears. Their defenses crumbled in confusion, and the Keriags swarmed over them. In seconds, the battle had become a free-for-all, friend and foe almost indistinguishable in the crush.

Ryushi searched frantically for Elani in the melee, but

he was forced to parry a slashing spear that came at him with enough force to jar his sword arm, and he had to return his concentration to the fight for a moment. Then Calica was there alongside him, her sword hacking and weaving faster than the eye could follow. Ryushi backed away, leaving Calica to her opponent, his thoughts occupied with —

Elani. She was over near the mouth of the steep, downward-sloping tunnel that gaped in the cave floor. She was backing away, her eyes wide with terror as a Keriag suddenly turned from the fray and fixed her with its stare. And then it began to skitter towards her.

Ryushi yelled, running across the cavern and leaping to intercept, his sword raised double-handed over his head. Elani screamed as she saw the Keriag lunging towards her; she instinctively tried to shift but she *couldn't*, because she was both surrounded by earth and high above the ground, and some sense inside her wouldn't allow her to risk the jump. And then Ryushi was swinging, meeting the creature in midair, scything through its forelegs and torso, chopping it almost in half. But the momentum of the Keriag could not be checked, and it slammed into Ryushi in a fountain of clear, sticky blood. He fell backward, flailing, his sword coming free, and knocked into Elani. With a shriek, she toppled over, and

149

he with her, and both of them went tumbling into the mouth of the pit at their feet.

"Fall back!" Calica yelled, her voice carrying over the tumult. "Fall back to the wyverns!"

"Which way?" somebody cried, desperate panic in their voice. "Which way? Where's the girl?"

"Elani? *Elani!*" This time it was Tochaa.

"I said fall back! We have to fall back!" Calica again.

But then, over the sound of the battle that raged around them, they heard another noise. At first it was a background sound, distant and rising and falling. But then it got louder, swelling until it equaled the volume of the clashes of sword on spear and the screams of the dying; and finally it overwhelmed them.

The shouting of men. The battle cries of Parakka.

The Parakkan troops burst into the cave, whooping and yelling, their weapons cleaving a bloody path through the rear ranks of the Keriags. The creatures were taken by surprise and vastly outnumbered, and they could do little to stop the onslaught of the human troops. Hochi grinned wildly, his hammer smashing this way and that, possessed by new strength. He swept forward to join them, a renewed battle-fury burning through his veins.

But he was careless. A Keriag, whom he had thought was dead after he brought his hammer across its skull, was only stunned. The blow had been glancing, and not nearly enough to finish it off. He stepped over it where it lay, and it lashed upwards with its spear, driving it deep into his upper leg. He bellowed in agony, his hammer swinging around to crush his assailant's head against the hard floor; but a moment later, his leg failed him, and he fell backward to the ground. Suddenly prone, his mind afire with pain, he saw the dark, spiderlike shape of another Keriag sweep into his vision, raising its spear above his body to finish him off.

The blow never came; for suddenly Tochaa was there, his left-hand knife knocking aside the shaft of the spear while the other stabbed through the Keriag's torso with a crunch. In seconds, another was on him, trying to get past him to the fallen form of Hochi, but the Kirin was steadfast, standing over the big man and holding the Keriags away. All around them, the Parakkan troops were demolishing what remained of the opposition, but they had not yet reached where Tochaa fought. Another Keriag appeared, then another, and in moments Tochaa was battling with three of them, his knives moving at incredible speed as he parried and stabbed, his lean body dodging between the vicious barbs of the *gaer bolga*.

151

Hochi watched in disbelief as the Kirin slashed one of them down, and before it had even crumpled he had wheeled and thrust his other knife into its companion's throat, and was turning to deal the fatal blow to the last one. . . .

"No!" Hochi cried out, his hand reaching out as if he could stop what he saw was happening. For the last Keriag had timed its thrust to perfection, and had anticipated where Tochaa was going to move to. Time seemed to slow to a crawl as Tochaa spun into the path of the awful spear, and it drove deep into his stomach. His eyes squeezed closed and his mouth fell open in a soundless gasp. And then, too late, the Parakkan troops were there, cleaving the Keriag from behind, and its chitin-rimmed hands loosened on the shaft of the spear as it crumpled.

But Tochaa was falling, falling, the terrible weapon lodged in his gut, his light armour already awash with red around the wound. He fell heavily next to Hochi with a brutal thump. The big man reached over with his huge arms, supporting the Kirin's shoulders and lifting his head up, his eyes full of horror and shock. The world around them, the orange dark of the cave, the milling of the Parakkan soldiers that were even now finishing off the last of the Keriags . . . they were nothing but a background buzz, incomprehensible and unimportant. It was as if Hochi and Tochaa were enclosed in a bubble, and only they existed inside it, while everything outside was blurred and vague.

"Tochaa . . ." Hochi said, the word little more than a whisper.

The Kirin's light eyes struggled open and looked at him. "This is my time, friend," he croaked. "I return to . . . the earth, to rejoin the Flow until . . ." He coughed, blood bubbling over his gray lips. "Until my rebirth."

"You saved me," Hochi said thickly, his eyes filling with tears.

"We . . . were both Elani's . . . uncles at one stage," the Kirin replied, a weak grin playing on his lips. "Doesn't that . . . make us brothers . . . of a sort?"

"Brothers," Hochi agreed, choked with emotion, his hand clasping tight over Tochaa's. "Brothers. By Cetra, I did you wrong. I never trusted you. You and your race. I did you *wrong*."

"I . . . have something for you," Tochaa said haltingly, fast weakening. "Around my neck. Take it . . . when I'm gone. Don't let . . . don't let Parakka die. Bring . . . bring it to . . . my people. Show them . . . how to be free."

"I will," Hochi promised, a tear falling down his cheek. "I will."

Tochaa's eyes flickered to the wound in Hochi's leg, where the spear still protruded, then back at his own spear and the deep red stain that soaked his clothes. He gasped a half laugh.

"We bleed . . . the same blood," he said, and died.

The tunnel was too steep to gain their feet and too shallow for a fall, and Ryushi and Elani were battered and bruised as they thumped and slid downwards. It was a terrifying feeling, to be a prisoner of their own momentum, unable to stop themselves rolling and skidding, hurtling through darkness towards who knew what. . . .

Their ordeal was brought to a sudden end as the tunnel spat them out onto a bed of packed earth, and they jarred and juddered to a bouncing halt. Ryushi's sword clattered down after. For a moment, neither of them moved. Then Elani began to sob.

Ryushi raised his head, wincing at the soreness there. The shaft had been mercifully short, but they had both been knocked about badly, and he ached in a hundred different places. Willing his reluctant muscles into action, he moved over to Elani and placed a hand on her shoulder, gathering her into him. She cried from the pain and the shock and the fear, and he soothed her, for despite all her inner strength she was still a child really.

As he did, he looked around this new place where they found themselves. It was another cavern, but this one was far larger than any they had previously seen inside the Warren. There was more light, too. It was bright in comparison to the rest of the chambers and tunnels they had encountered, although that still didn't amount to much. But the glowstones here were white, not the usual orange that mangled colors to dark greens and blacks. And all around the cavern were purples and blues, yellows, and reds, huge, gently stirring puffs of fungus that covered the earthen walls. Most of them stood at least three times his height, like enormous, misshapen sponges. And as he looked longer, he saw a strange kind of organization in the way that the sponges were laid out, and he realized that they were standing on the edge of a garden. An enormous, underground fungus garden.

"El," he whispered. "El, look at this."

Tearfully, she stirred in his arms and looked around.

"It's amazing," he said. "The Keriags must live on this stuff, and cultivate it themselves."

"Cousin Ryushi," Elani said. "It's starting."

"What's starting?" he asked automatically, and then felt a sudden sinking dread as he realized the answer to his own question.

"Macaan has everything in place. He must know how we've gotten into one of his Warrens. He's starting it. The Integration."

Ryushi got hastily to his feet, scooping her up with him. She moaned a quiet "Owww," as her bruises throbbed, but no more. He picked up his sword where it had fallen and sheathed it.

"Where is it?" he demanded. "We gotta stop it!"

"It's near," she said. "Through there somewhere." She motioned at the fungus garden.

"Well, come on, then!" Ryushi said urgently.

He began to run, ignoring the protests of his battered body, heading through the hulking fungus crops towards the other side of the cavern, where Elani had pointed. As he neared, he could see the top edge of a tunnel mouth over a ridge of puffballs.

"Is that it?" he asked breathlessly.

"I think so," Elani said wearily. "Yeah, it must be." She was tired, and aching, and she felt a sudden, overwhelming urge just to bury her head in Ryushi's chest and sleep. Her eyes had closed in exhaustion when she felt Ryushi slow suddenly, and come to a stop. Gently, he lowered her down, and she slipped out of his arms onto her feet, looking around to see what was the cause.

She didn't have to look far. Standing at the tunnel entrance was a warrior, clad in ornate green armour that was molded to his slim, lean figure. Upon his face he wore a mask of silver, fashioned in the shape of a screaming spirit, and his dark hair hung in a long pony-tail down his back. He held a curved nodachi sword before him, and his stance suggested that he knew well how to use it.

It was the warrior who had killed Kia's and Ryushi's father.

The long, drawn-out *sshhhrrik* of Ryushi's blade being unsheathed sounded through the silent cavern.

"One of us," he said grimly, "is not leaving this place alive."

"I wouldn't have it any other way," replied his opponent, and he reached up to pull off his silver mask with one hand. It fell to the floor with a short, tinny crash.

The tip of Ryushi's sword began to tremble. His throat seemed to close up. His head began to pound, as if his skull could not contain the enormity of what he saw. And in that moment, he knew everything. The killer of their father. The betrayer of Parakka. The one who had destroyed their lives.

Takami.

His brother.

Takami.

4

Not Just Black and White

"Why?"

The word came out as a strangled gasp. Ryushi's eyes pleaded with the one who stood before him, begging him to make some sense of it all.

"Really, little brother, you always were annoyingly curious," Takami said, cocking his head to one side and studying Ryushi as if he were an amusing pet. "Does there have to be a *why*?"

"But . . . Father . . . Aunt Susa . . . you would have killed *us*!" Ryushi forced the words out past his shock-numbed mouth.

"Yes, and I have to admit to being *impressed*, little brother. Your escape was so dramatic. Unfortunately, your and Kia's continued existence did somewhat crimp my victory. I did intend to have the whole family executed at a stroke, but you went and made things awkward and I had to go ahead without you and my other delightful sibling. No matter." He smiled nastily. "We'll soon rectify that minor slip."

"Tell me why, Takami," Ryushi said, his voice gathering strength as he slowly began to accept the evidence his eyes and ears had put before him. "Before I kill you. Tell me why."

Takami raised an eyebrow. "You are a persistent one, I'll give you that," he said. "And optimistic, too." He shrugged. "Maybe I don't feel like telling you. I think it'd be better if you died never knowing. It adds a certain extra hint of tragedy to the whole affair."

His nodachi held two-handed across his body, he began to slowly advance, moving gracefully on the balls of his feet, his weight balanced perfectly. Ryushi put a hand on Elani's shoulder and moved her behind him, readying his own weapon.

"Get back, El," he said, his voice dry as ashes.

"Cousin Ryushi, it's beginning. . . ." she reminded him.

"I know," he replied. He was acutely aware that time was short, and that he had to get this over with quickly if they were to have any hope of stopping the King and his daughter. But first, he would know the answers to the questions burning inside him.

They closed to within striking distance of each other and held their stances, their eyes locked.

"You *are* drearily predictable," Takami said wearily. "From the moment I heard you'd been seen in the company of that fat fool Hochi, I knew we'd meet like this. Just couldn't resist Parakka, could you? Don't you know you never had a *choice*? Father was bringing us up to be shoehorned into his little pet rebellion ever since we were born."

The tips of their swords hovered together, less than an inch apart.

"That may be true," Ryushi replied. "But what was the alternative? Macaan? The one who'd killed my family? Don't try and be clever, Takami. It was *you* who drove me to Parakka, by betraying us. Not Father. You. You're lower than filth."

"Oho! So it seems the little brother has forgotten his *place*!" With the last word, Takami flicked Ryushi's sword aside and made a swift jab at his chest, but Ryushi sidestepped in the blink of an eye and knocked his brother's weapon away. In less than a moment, they had returned to their original positions, facing each other levelly.

160

"So what about you?" Ryushi asked. "What did Macaan give you to choose his side?"

"He offered me nothing," Takami said. "I *demanded*. I saw what was happening in the Dominions. When Father took me with him to Tusami City, I learned enough from the whining of Parakka to know which way the tide was going."

"You chose Macaan," Ryushi stated bluntly.

"I chose the winning side. Better that than to align myself with our father's foolish dream, or to be one of the meek in the middle."

"And you saw a way to get yourself in with the King," Ryushi continued, his words bleeding scorn. "By forsaking your family, your childhood, and your honor. Was it worth it?"

"Oh yes," Takami said with a cold smile. "Indisputably."

Their swords blurred and clashed with a ring that echoed throughout the cavern. Ryushi slashed low, aiming for Takami's legs, but his brother parried and spun, sending a chop at his neck that would behead him. Ryushi ducked it smoothly, jabbing the hilt of his sword into Takami's stomach, but there was rigid armour there and the blow did little. High, low, their weapons chimed again and again as they swung and dodged,

161

stabbed and blocked; and finally they parted, resuming their original stances, their sword points an inch apart.

"And what did you . . . *demand* from Macaan?" Ryushi said, continuing the conversation as if there had never been a break.

"Father always did place too much trust in his children," Takami replied, not in the least out of breath. "He took me to Tusami City, and he told me about Parakka, and who he was. I expect you know he founded it?" Ryushi nodded tersely. "Well, he wanted to persuade me to join his cause. He took me to Hochi; he showed me some of the safehouses in the city. He told me about Gar Jenna, but not, unfortunately, where it was. He was desperate to have me see things his way. Fool." Takami paused. "I exchanged all the information I had on Parakka and its operatives for a title. Land. *Power*, little brother. Are you proud of me? You should be. Your elder sibling is now the Thane of the province of Maar in Kirin Taq, a member of Princess Aurin's court. I am Takami-*kos*! A noble!"

"Noble?" Ryushi spat. "I doubt it."

Another short, punching ring as Takami stabbed and Ryushi, with a quick movement, knocked his blade aside. They returned to their ready positions, sidestepping slowly, circling each other.

"So why?" Ryushi asked. "Why do it? What had we done . . . what had Father done to make you betray us? You told me what you got. Now tell me why you did it."

"You really can't take no for an answer, can you?" Takami asked, almost incredulous. "Why can't you accept that it was just my naked ambition, that I'm evil at heart? That's what you want to hear, isn't it? Save me a lengthy explanation that you might not *survive* to hear the end of."

"Because that's not all," Ryushi replied. "You've only told me half of it. Real life isn't that simple. It's not just black and white."

"Real *life*?" Takami laughed. "What do *you* know of real life? Little brother, I'm really going to miss your sense of humor."

His blade suddenly lashed outward, slicing at Ryushi's belly. It came so close that Elani squealed, thinking it had disemboweled him; but Ryushi had pulled himself back, and it had missed by a hair's breadth. He struck in response, hard; Takami's parry barely stood up to the force of his swing. For a moment, a flicker of concern crossed the older brother's face, but the next instant it was gone as he turned his blade to meet another swing, cutting inward at a lethal angle. Ryushi sent another one at his head, turning it at the last

163

moment towards his arm instead, and once more Takami only just managed to turn the blade aside; but the force of it was enough to make him stagger back and away, to get some breathing space. A frond of hair had escaped his ponytail and was hanging over his face.

"You've gotten better, little brother," he commended, and Ryushi noticed that he was breathing harder with the exertion now. "But I'll wager, not better than me yet."

"Stake your life on that?" Ryushi countered.

The amusement drained out of his brother's face, replaced by anger. "It's not my life that will be lost today," he said.

"What's the matter, *brother*?" Ryushi sneered. "Is it not so *funny* anymore?"

And with that, he suddenly lunged into an attack, feinting a swipe and then going for a stab at Takami's throat. Takami got his blade up in time to deflect it, but not enough; the tip of Ryushi's sword cut deep into his shoulder, and he cried out in pain. But Ryushi did not give him a second to recover; he swung another blow at his brother, and again, and again, raining strikes on Takami so that he had barely a chance to parry one attack before another one was coming. He backed off under the force of Ryushi's anger, steadily giving ground, retreating through the mouth of the short tunnel he had emerged from.

"You know what?" Ryushi was saying through gritted teeth as he hammered against his brother's sword, attacking hard and viciously but never leaving himself exposed. "I don't *need* your justifications. Was it because you were jealous of the way me and Kia always had each other, and that you were always alone? Was it that you hated Father because he made you train, made you *special*, made you an outcast like we were . . . but you had no one to share the burden with? Did you hate Parakka because Mother *died* for them, and you blamed Father for it? Or was it all of that? Is that what *twisted* you, so that when you saw a chance to seize power, no matter what the cost, you *took* it?" With this last sentence, he smashed a blow down on Takami's sword, and it jarred out of his hand and flew away as he staggered backward and tripped, landing heavily on the floor, glaring at Ryushi. "It doesn't matter," he said, more softly. "You did it. Now you're gonna pay."

Their fight had taken them through the tunnel and into the cavern on the other side, and all at once Ryushi realized where they were. The heart of the Ley Warren. The air around them seemed thick with power; it whined in their ears, and forced itself down their throats

165

and nostrils. In the center of the circular cavern was an immense machine, a towering cone of metal that tapered towards the top, disappearing into the gloom. It was hugely complex, its surface covered by thousands of thin pipes, valves, and protrusions of all kinds. But Ryushi saw with horror that there were *people* inside that construction, meshed with the iron, half buried at apparently random positions all the way up the body of the machine. Here the pink of a thigh and knee showed through; there a face was covered by a grim metal visor, with only the chin and throat visible; elsewhere, a bare foot was encased in a metal pedal-slipper. These were Resonants, entrapped by Macaan and forced to become part of his monstrous machine; and if Ryushi had ever had any remaining doubts about his decision to join Parakka, they vanished then.

Takami saw the expression on his brother's face, and his features twisted into a cruel smile. "Magnificent, isn't it? A Ley Booster. One in each Warren. It took thousands of Machinists to build them all. And it took a while to round up all the *volunteers* to power it. But look at that thing, and tell me it wasn't all worth it."

"Ryushi, we have to *stop* it!" Elani insisted. She had followed them in.

+++ You cannot stop it. It has begun. +++

Ryushi didn't turn away from where Takami lay on the floor, but he saw the shape of the Jachyra out of the corner of his eye, slinking from the shadows around the base of the Ley Booster. He guessed that where there was a Jachyra, there would be some kind of mirror nearby to use as a portal, but the light was too dim and foiled his attempts to find one.

+++ Your resistance is in vain. +++ said the buzzing voice of Tatterdemalion. **+++ The Integration cannot be stopped now. The invasion will commence. The Dominions will fall under the command of King Macaan. Surrender yourself and the girl, and you will live. +++**

"Stay out of this," said Takami. "This isn't finished yet." He turned his eyes to Ryushi. "Well, little brother? Are you going to kill me here, on the floor, or shall we finish this with honor?"

Ryushi hesitated for a moment, his cheeks burning with hatred. But even after all his brother had done, he could not bring himself to slay him as he was defenseless. Even if Takami had forsaken his honor long ago, that only made it doubly important to Ryushi that he keep his. He stepped back and allowed Takami to rise and reclaim his nodachi.

+++ Takami-kos, reinforcements are on the way. The Parakkan forces will have to retreat. They do not have

the numbers to hold this place against us. Further risk to yourself is — +++

"Stay *out* of this," Takami shouted. "This is something to be settled between *family*."

"You're no family of mine," Ryushi grated. "Not anymore. And we'll *see* whether or not that machine can be stopped. But first . . ." He dropped into a ready stance. "Let's see how good you really are."

"Oh, you will," Takami promised, and he charged with a yell, his sword swinging downwards. It ignited in his hands, fired by his spirit-stones, carving a path of sluggish ocher flames through the gloom. Ryushi back-flipped away from him, spinning once in the air and landing catlike on his feet an instant before jumping the low sweep Takami sent at his ankles. Takami rolled out of the way of his counterstrike, coming to his feet in one fluid motion and thrusting his hand out. A blast of thick greenish flames burst from his hand, slamming into Ryushi; but his brother held his sword across him and threw up his defenses, digging in his feet. Takami's assault continued for several long seconds, pounding at Ryushi's shields, and even though he leaned into it he felt his boots sliding backward across the hard earth, carving little furrows as he went.

A moment later, the fire retreated. Takami was standing there, his self-confident smirk back on his face, his ponytailed hair now in disarray. Sweat shone on his cheeks, and one hand still ran with flame, green tongues flickering around the gloved fingers. Both of them were breathing heavily.

"I see you've improved all around, little brother," Takami said. "Not many could have stood up so well to my fire. But what of *your* powers? Why do you hold back? Could it be that you *still* can't control your stones? That you still drain yourself totally whenever you let them loose? Oh, that *is* a shame." His voice dropped, becoming more serious. "You should have killed me when I was on the floor. Your precious honor will only win you death."

Ryushi's eyes flickered around the cavern. Tatterdemalion was still watching from the shadows, hunched over, his glassy eyes reflecting the faint light. He was making no move towards Elani, who cowered near the tunnel entrance, watching the Jachyra nervously. Perhaps the girl was of no interest to them, now that the Integration had begun. He was aware, also, of an increasing whine that had started to come from the Ley Booster.

End this, he thought. *End it quickly!*

"Time to die, little brother," Takami said, and his

whole body exploded in flame as he threw the full force of his stones against Ryushi. Ryushi buckled under the relentless fire, curving and licking around the protective bubble he threw up around himself, engulfing him in its roar and scorching him with its heat. He was forced to his knees, trembling as if under an enormous weight. His arm up in front of his face, he felt his defenses beginning to crumble, for Takami was strong, so *strong,* and any second the eerie green fire would rush in and consume him.

And then who'll protect Elani? Who'll keep my promise to Father?

He gritted his teeth and began to rise again. Shuddering against the awesome, howling force that blasted at him, Ryushi made himself rise, slowly, fighting every inch of the way, until he was back on his feet.

"Fall down, curse you!" Takami shrieked. "*Fall!*"

"Is that . . . the *best* . . . you can do?" Ryushi said, his voice straining with the effort. Through the sheets of flames, he looked into his brother's eyes. "Counterstrike."

The Flow burst through him, released at last, searing through his veins and blasting out of his hand in a tight, focused beam of force, cutting through the center of Takami's fire and striking him square in the chest. Too late, Takami tried to throw up his own defenses, but he had not been ready for the attack and he could put up little resistance. It smashed into him, a screaming explosion of energy following in its wake, sending him flying across the cavern, his arms and legs flailing, and hurled him into the Ley Booster. Ryushi saw him bring up a protective shield a split second before impact, and then he careered into the machine.

The explosion of the collision was immense, a shock wave of concussion and green fire that swept outward across the cavern. Ryushi flung himself onto Elani, sheltering her with his body and encasing them in his defenses as the blast howled over them, their eyes squeezed tight shut. . . .

And then silence.

The cavern was in near darkness. All but a few of the glowstones in the walls had smashed, their illumination dead. The Ley Booster was misshapen, its towering body a buckled shadow. At its foot, there was the dark lump of a body: Takami's. Alive, doubtless. But defeated.

Ryushi shook his head, his dirtied blond quills shaking with it. He took a heavy, shuddering breath. Beneath him, Elani gave a quizzical whimper, as if surprised that she was still there.

But where was the Jachyra?

The Ley Booster began to hum again, a different tone now, an unpleasant buzzing that gradually gathered in volume, faded, returned louder, faded again, and then came back, louder and louder.

"It's still trying to activate!" Elani said. "Cousin Ryushi. Get up!"

+++ He cannot get up. +++ said a voice from the darkness, followed by a short crackle. **+++ He has drained himself, just as Takami-kos said. +++**

Elani's eyes searched the heavy gloom, fixing suddenly on the sight of the thin, rag-swathed figure of Tatterdemalion coming slowly, cautiously towards her, crouching low.

"Stay away!" she shrieked.

+++ But your protector is powerless, Resonant. Who is there to make me? King Macaan will enjoy meeting you, after all the trouble you have caused him. And the Jachyra owe a special debt to this one, for what he did to one of our comrades. +++

"And unless you want to go the same way, I'd listen to the girl," Ryushi said. Both of them turned to look at him, and Elani gasped as she saw him beginning to rise to his feet. Teeth gritted, sweat breaking on his brow, he picked himself up. First he got to his knees, then he slid one foot under him, and finally, shakily, he stood up, facing the creature. "Are you so sure that Takami was right?"

Tatterdemalion hesitated, his telescopic eye whirring.
+++ **You are bluffing.** +++

"Wanna find out? Try to take Elani and see." Ryushi looked at the Jachyra squarely. In the background, the hum of the Ley Booster was becoming a deafening drone, making the floor tremble. A few stones shook loose from the ceiling of the cavern. Tatterdemalion studied him, seeming to disbelieve him but not so certain of himself that he was willing to take on Ryushi in a straight fight, if he turned out to be wrong. The lenses of his eyes turned slowly from him to Elani and back again.

+++ **There will be a reckoning.** +++ he promised.
+++ **For both of you.** +++

And with that, he turned and went over to where Takami lay in shadow, picking him up with a strength that belied his thin, emaciated body. Elani clutched Ryushi's hand as they watched him take the fallen betrayer to the same shadowed nook that he had emerged from, to whatever secret portal lay within.

+++ **There is nowhere to run from us.** +++ the Jachyra said, his voice a mechanical hiss of static; and then he was gone, his burden with him, and they were left with

173

only the terrible, ascending hum of the damaged Ley Booster.

Ryushi's knees buckled the second their enemies were out of sight. He staggered and nearly fell, but Elani tugged him upright again.

"You really *were* bluffing," she said. "But I thought you drained yourself completely."

"Not completely," he said. "This time . . . I held a little back." He turned a weak smile on her. "Guess I'm improving."

"Can you run, Cousin Ryushi?"

"I can run," he replied.

"I don't wanna be next to that thing when the Integration happens," she said, glancing at the Ley Booster. "Let's get out of here!"

"You know the way? Back to the wyverns?"

"Course I do!" she said impatiently. "You think I'd bring you all the way in here if I couldn't find my way back?"

Ryushi even managed a laugh as they stumbled away, Elani dragging him by his hand while he staggered after, into the depths of the tunnels.

Outside, the battle still raged.

The breach in the red, earthen wall of the Warren that

Ty had made with the Bear Claw had become littered with corpses: Guardsmen, Keriags, and Parakkans alike had fallen there. The fighting was desperate; the Parakkan forces were many times outnumbered, but they held a highly defensible position, and three of the enemy fell to each one of theirs. The gargantuan mukhili and the tanned desert-folk combined with the war machines from the West to form an impenetrable barrier, which the Keriags could not break through. The Parakkan wyverns that had survived the initial assault on the Warren now swept over the black tide of the enemy, punching bolts of concussion from their force-cannons into the mass of bodies.

But the defenders were steadily declining in number, and those that were left were flagging badly, while the attackers seemed endless and inexhaustible.

There was no warning when the change happened. The Ley Warren was humming and shaking, that much was true, sending occasional landslides of earth down its sides and on to the battle below. But it had been doing that for some time when the Keriags suddenly stopped fighting.

A silence fell over the battlefield. The defenders did not know what to make of it. Nor did the Guardsmen who fought alongside the creatures. They just *stopped*, all of them, together, at exactly the same moment.

And then they began to retreat.

First it was one, the tapping of its hooklike feet rising above the ranks as it slowly backed away. Then there were more, the Keriags keeping a wary eye on the Parakkan troops as their six spiderlike legs carried them away. And finally, as one, the remaining creatures turned and ran, skittering away in one enormous mass, one huge unanimous movement. There was no panic or confusion; though they were pressed tightly together, they never impeded one another. But they ran; and the Guardsmen, seeing what was happening, began to retreat with them, turning their vehicles around and leaving the battlefield, heading away across the hot veldt.

For a moment, there was no reaction from the Parakkan troops.

And then there was a cheer, so long and loud that it echoed through the tunnels and chambers of the Ley Warren, chasing its way up to the tips of the spires.

Darkness. Pain.

Ty slowly became aware of where he was. In the close confines of the Bear Claw's cockpit, the blackness was total. No light came in through the viewing-port, buried as it was under tons of earth. His face was wet, and the air was heavy with the hot, sticky scent of blood. Next to him, he could sense the presence of Otomo, slumped at a bad angle, unmoving. Was he breathing? He couldn't tell.

But something had stirred him. Something. An urgent call on his mind that had pulled him from unconsciousness. What, though? What could it —

There, again. A rumbling, a scraping . . . hundreds of stones skittering across the metal of the Bear Claw's roof, as if driven by some force . . .

Then the sound of dull, tinny rapping on the hatch in the roof of the cockpit.

For a moment, Ty was still, his head tilted dumbly upwards in the darkness, unable to understand what it might mean. Then, as his mind cleared, he realized someone was outside, on the roof of the Claw. But surely that was impossible; hadn't he *buried* it? Or maybe it hadn't been as bad as he had thought?

What if it's the Keriags? What if it's the Guardsmen?

He didn't care. He had no choice. If he didn't open that hatch, he and Otomo were going to die in here. If the bigger man wasn't dead already.

The rapping again.

He reached up, blindly groping, forcing his body to fight the curiously immense pull of gravity that resisted him, and found the release catch. With a final effort, he jerked his wrist and it came free, the hatch popping open with a hiss of pressure, letting in a square of faint light.

And then, reaching in for him was Kia; he felt her arms around his arms, smelled her scent, recognized her shape even if he couldn't see her. She held him in an awkward hug, he half managing to stand and she hanging through the hatch. And even though he was injured and disoriented, he could feel something was wrong with her. She trembled as if she were palsied, and her muscles jumped erratically.

But she held him, and kissed him, and then withdrew as people reached past her, people Ty had not seen before, and began to help him out of his metal coffin.

The Keriags were deserting the Warren. Like animals that could sense an earthquake long before it happened, those members of the Princess's army that still remained in the labyrinthine tunnels knew what was coming and fled. Ryushi and Elani had long since given up trying to hide from them; the Keriags scuttled past the pair as if they were not there at all, ignoring them completely. Instead, they stumbled and staggered onward, back toward the place where they had left the wyverns. All around them, the earthen tunnel walls shook and shuddered. The hum of the Ley Booster continued to rise maddeningly, terrifyingly. They did not know what would happen when the damaged machine attempted to take its part in the Integration, but they did not dare risk being close enough to find out when it did.

So they ran, Ryushi pushing his tortured body to its limit in an attempt to keep up with Elani, who led him confidently through the maze, shying away from the Keriags that passed them by. Each step seemed to take an age, and there seemed to be no end in sight. He was exhausted, unconscious on his feet, and only operating on automatic until he heard:

"Ryushi! Elani!"

It was Calica. Her katana in one hand, she appeared ahead of them, half lit in the orange glow. Running up to them, she sheathed her weapon and slung a supporting arm around Ryushi's shoulders. He slumped into her, burying his face in the cascade of her hair. "Hochi!" she called up the corridor. "They're here!" And a moment later, Hochi's strong arms were also bearing him up, and together they staggered the last stretch to where the sunlight blazed in through the rent in the Warren that Kia had made. One wyvern remained there, regarding the newcomers with its amber eyes, shuffling anxiously as it felt the shaking of the Warren's death throes.

179

Hochi, grim-faced, lifted Ryushi up into a harness while Calica secured the straps around him, then did the same for Elani, who was urging him to hurry. When that was done, they mounted up and Hochi took control of the creature, his practiced hands turning it about so that it faced the sun. It took two short hops forward and then sprang on its powerful legs, launching them into the sky, its four wings spreading out to either side of them. The immense Warren spread out beneath them as they sailed between its shuddering and crumbling spires, battered by the enormous bass drone of its malfunctioning heart; and then it fell away behind them, and they could see the ragged remains of the Parakkan army on the veldt, sallying away from the structure before it became too unstable.

"Go! Get us out of here!" Calica was yelling at Hochi, who was spurring the wyvern on as fast as it could go.

"It's too late," Elani said quietly.

And behind them, the Ley Warren erupted.

It was not an explosion. It was not like anything ever seen before in the Dominions. What it *was*, was the raw power of the ley lines, the brutal, naked Flow that the Ley Booster had tapped but was unable to contain be-

cause it had been damaged. The Warren bulged outward, seeming to warp and expand for a split second,
then gathered rapidly in on itself like a crumpled scroll,
diminishing to nothing, nothing except a pinprick-sized
hole in the worlds. . . .

And then the loosed energy blasted outward, a terrific,
blue, crackling wave that seared away from the epicenter,
a huge expanding circle, racing wider and wider across
the veldt in a wall of pure Flow a mile high. Elani
screamed as she saw it rushing towards them, but she had
no more than a second before it hit, sweeping over them,
through them, seeming to penetrate every fiber of their
being and scouring along it; and it engulfed the retreating
Parakkan army, too, ground and air, swallowing everything, *everything*. . . .

And then it snuffed out, and all was peace.

Hochi, Calica, Ryushi, and Elani were still flying, the
calm air stirring their hair, the wyvern's wingbeats slowing to a cruising speed. Beneath them, what was left of
Parakka was still there, also, crawling along the plains of
dark blue-black, between the outcrops of delicate, almost crystalline trees. Against the cool purple sky, the
rest of the Parakkan wyverns hung, gliding.

Elani looked up, tilting her head to the sky, her black
hair shucking from her small shoulders; and there hung

the great black disc, surrounded by its blazing, slowly moving corona.

"Tweentime," she whispered.

"Kirin Taq," Calica agreed.

The soft wind whispered across the empty, twilight plains, and the wyvern made a strange noise, deep in its thick throat.

Of the Keriags, and of Macaan's Guardsmen, there was nothing to be seen.

5

A Hundred of Your Kind

Hochi sat, cross-legged, on the grassy stone ridge. Below him, nestled in the crook of the hills and the delicate blue shimmer of the Kirin Taq forest, campfires burned and shadows moved. The decimated army of Parakka was licking its wounds, treating its casualties, counting its losses. Hiding. As they always had.

Hochi was motionless, his huge shoulders slumped under his thin hemp shirt, his thick arms crossed in his lap. The faint light from the eclipsed sun threw half his face into deeper shadow. Above, wispy wine-colored clouds drifted slowly away from him.

After a time, he was aware of the soft tread of boots on the turf, coming up behind. There was a rustle as the

newcomer sat down on his right, sharing his high perch.
He didn't turn to look who it was. He didn't need to.

"We failed," he stated flatly.

Calica made a noise of reluctant concession next to
him, as if to say: *If that's how you want to see it . . .*

"Well, we did, didn't we?" he said, suddenly stirred
to faint anger by her response. "All we did was stop
one of the Warrens working the way it was supposed to.
You saw how much power it put out. The others will
have worked just fine. Macaan got his Integration. Right
now, thousands upon thousands of those cursed black
monstrosities are pouring out of every Ley Warren in
the Dominions. Nobody even knows they're coming.
You can't defend against those things, not that many of
them. That's it. The end. We lost. He won, he and his
daughter. . . ."

"The fight goes on, Hochi," Calica said, brushing a
strand of hair behind her ear. "It's not over."

"It *is* over," the big man growled, his eyes flashing
darkly in frustration as he looked at her. "We couldn't
beat the smallest part of his army with five thousand
troops. We've got perhaps a fifth of that now. A thousand —"

"A thousand troops that both Macaan and Princess
Aurin will think are *dead*," Calica interrupted. "And the

dead move much more quietly than the living, don't you think?"

Hochi was silent for a moment. Then, begrudging her the point, he said, "You don't know the mind of Macaan."

"I know it better than anybody, Hochi. I've *been* there, remember? Look, nobody knew what would happen when that damaged Ley Booster went up. I'm *still* not sure how it worked; even Elani couldn't say, and she's a Resonant. My best guess is that whatever power it was that was supposed to make the Ley Warren exist in both worlds at once, to become a crossing-point, got released when the Booster blew and hit us. We got lucky. All it did was shift us into Kirin Taq." She paused, to see if anything she was saying was getting through to him. "But listen, Hochi, none of the King's troops or the Keriags got shifted with us. That meant that whatever happened, they were out of its range of effect. They stayed in the Dominions."

"It must have seemed as if we were just wiped off the veldt," Hochi said slowly. "Just disappeared."

"Right," Calica said. "That makes a thousand dead men and women we've got camping below us, not to mention machines and mukhili and pakpaks and so on. This isn't the end. It's just a setback. 'Cause Macaan's and Aurin's eyes are going to be on the Dominions for a long time to come, until he's got them all under his glove. And that means their forces will be there, too. And *that* means —"

"We rebuild!" Hochi said, a hint of excitement in his voice. "While he's concerned with the Dominions, we rebuild Parakka in Kirin Taq! If he thinks he's wiped us out, he won't suspect a thing."

"Until it's too late," Calica finished, a smile curving her lips.

Hochi scratched the top of his boot. "You always had the gift of words, Calica."

She shrugged lightly. "I'd rather have yours."

"Mine? I don't *have* one."

"No? How many people have you ever met who've got to where you were with your start in life, Hochi? How many who had owned a thriving wyvern Stud, who'd fought so many battles and lived, who'd made such a success of themselves without ever possessing so much as a single spirit-stone? Your parents were so poor, they couldn't afford even one. A hundred such people are born and die in poverty every day. But you *didn't*." She laid her hand on the back of his arm. "Now stop feeling sorry for yourself."

186

There was a short silence, as they both watched the velvet sky.

"How are the others?" he asked at length.

Calica sighed. "Ty and Kia are both very bad. She almost killed herself taking out all those force-cannons, and she made it worse when she dug Ty out. She drained herself and then some. I've never seen anything like it." She looked at him. "Our healers are treating them. They say there's a good chance they'll pull through." Her eyes dropped to the ground. "Otomo didn't make it."

"The troops think they're heroes," Hochi said. "Ryushi, too. What victory we have, we owe mainly to them."

Calica looked sad for a moment. "Ryushi sits silently by their sickbeds, with Elani in his lap. He's hardly said a word. I'm worried about him. After what he discovered about his brother . . ."

"We all have our scars," Hochi said. "The only thing I fear is that we will have many more before this is all over."

His words fell into another silence, both of them considering what he had said.

Then Calica stirred. "Don't stay up here alone. There's people who want to see you. Maybe you should go to Elani. She lost one of her uncles today. She needs to know that the other one is still around."

"In a moment," Hochi said.

Calica smiled understandingly, then got to her feet and left, the sound of her boots fading behind her.

For a long minute, Hochi sat there, cross-legged, thinking. His hands toyed with the pendant that hung around his neck on a thin metal chain. It was wrought in silver, in the image of the corona of the Kirin Taq sun. Set in the hollow center was a symbol, finely crafted in smooth, curving lines. What it meant, Hochi did not know. But this was what Tochaa had given him in his last moments, and it bore with it a responsibility that he could not yet even guess at.

Don't let Parakka die. Bring it to my people. Show them how to be free.

A Kirin, a man he had mistrusted even though he had never been given any reason to do so, had said those words to him. In the face of Hochi's groundless dislike, that man had still called him a brother. It made him ashamed. And he needed to atone for that shame.

He got to his feet, standing against the twilight sky of an alien world, and weighed the small gift in his huge hand.

Don't let Parakka die. Bring it to my people. Show them how to be free.

"I will, brother," Hochi said quietly, and then tucked the pendant back in his shirt and walked down to rejoin the others.

The Integration has taken place and King Macaan has won. What lies ahead for Parakka? Find out in . . .

Broken Sky

Coming Soon

Kia drew the Glimmer shard from her belt and looked at it. The pulse at its core flashed a weak browny-red. She'd had this shard for too long; it would soon be time to get another.

"Are we on time?" Ryushi asked, standing next to her.

"I'm not sure. It's so hard to be exact with these things," she replied.

Their meeting-point with Taacqan was a sheltered spot underneath a rocky bluff that hung over their heads. They were surrounded by a sparse smattering of many-armed wychwood trees, their circular blue leaves layered like scales along their limbs. The dark sun brooded in the narrow slash of sky between the treetops and the lip of the stone overhang, watching them.

"I don't like this," Ryushi commented.

"He's not even late yet," Calica said, from where she leaned against the rock wall behind them, turning her katana in the dim light and examining its edge. "You're just having a paranoid day." Calica still hadn't gotten out of the Dominion habit of referring to day and night; in fact, she maintained it on purpose, as if reluctant to forsake the ways of her homeland.

"We could have chosen a better place than this," Jaan said darkly. "It's well-hidden enough, but it'd be perfect if they decided to ambush us."

"You kidding?" Calica said. She tapped Ryushi on the arm with the flat of her blade. "Our little supernova here could clear the forest for half a mile in any direction if it came to a fight. Anyway, these people are sailors and fishermen, not warriors."

"You sound very confident, Calica," Peliqua said.

"Call it intuition," she replied slyly, "but I've got a feeling Taacqan is going to turn up real soon. Alone. And he's picked up a bit of a cold since last time we saw him."

Nobody argued with her; her spirit-stones worked both ways, past *and* future, and she had a disconcerting habit of predicting things that were about to occur. This time was no exception; she had barely finished her sentence before they heard the sound of branches being pushed aside and the soft pad of footsteps on the turf. A few moments later, Taacqan appeared, sneezing explosively as he arrived.

"My apologies," he said. "I've picked up —"

"— *a bit of a cold since last time we saw you*," Peliqua and Ryushi chorused, grinning. Calica shrugged in the background. "Lucky guess," she said, and went back to the nonchalant examination of her blade.

Taacqan frowned, aware that there was some joke going on that he didn't understand, but he decided it wasn't worth pursuing and said: "Are you all ready? The others are waiting nearby."

"Lead us, then," Kia said, pulling her bo staff up from where she had been leaning on it and casting a disparaging glance at Calica.

South of the border of the Unclaimed Lands, the wetland foliage changed to forests of wychwood and haaka, which petered out as they reached the rocky shores and cliffs of the coast around Mon Tetsaa. It was through these forests that Taacqan took them, avoiding the open land in case they should be spotted by the King's Riders on wyvern-back. As a rule, the Riders did not come this far north, tending to stay in the more populous provinces inland, but Taacqan was nervous enough as it was and was in no mood to take chances.

"What happens when you've met the others?" Taacqan asked suddenly, looking at Kia.

"Well, once they've gotten over the fact that we're Dominion-born —" Kia began, but Taacqan interrupted with: "Oh, I told them that already."

"How did they take it?"

"Two dropped out. They said they wouldn't trust their lives to Dominion-folk. The rest are . . . um . . . wary, but they still want to join. They'll come around more fully when they've had time to think. It was just a bit of a shock. I mean, first the halfbreed and now you four . . ."

"We can't pick and choose our members, Taacqan," Kia said, a little sternly. "All that's necessary is the will to resist the tyranny you live under. Anything else is purely cosmetic."

Taacqan was silent for a time, leading them through the trees without ever seeming to need to check where he was, sniffing occasionally because his nose was running. Then, at last, he spoke: "We want to learn more," he said slowly. "*I* want to learn more, be of use to you. Against Aurin."

"Then you're welcome," Kia replied. "And if your friends feel the same, we'll take it from there. What you can do depends on your individual skills. Some might be of use to us staying here, being our eyes among the Marginals. Others we might need at one of our sanctuaries. It depends."

The trees began to thin out now, dissolving into the jagged rocks, coves, and inlets of the coast. The ground was covered in scrub and shale, and their footsteps changed from thuds to crunches as they made their way down to another cove, this one even smaller and more well-hidden than the one they had first met in. Mon Tetsaa was a distant clump of lights to the north, just visible below the horizon. Here, all was silent but for the susurrant hiss of the waves and the fitful sighs of the wind.

The descent to the cove was, if anything, even rougher than the last one. The rocks slanted sharply down towards the beach, and water runoff from the higher ground had carved shallow trenches into the stone that made the footing precarious. There was no campfire here, but Jaan and Peliqua, with their keener vision, could make out the group of waiting figures on the black sand below. Eventually, the Parakkans touched down on the beach and strode across towards Taacqan's companions. One of the figures broke away from the main group to meet them. He was unusually stocky for a Kirin, with a close-cut beard of dark blue and heavy brows above his striking white eyes.

"Taacqan," he said gruffly. "These are the Parakkans?"

Taacqan introduced them each in turn, ending with the newcomer, whose name was Aran. "I didn't think you were coming," Taacqan said to his companion. "I hoped my message had reached you."

"Not before time, either," Aran replied. "A day later and I would have been on my way south again, down the coast." He paused. "I'm sorry for your brother, Taacqan: I heard you put up a good fight before they dragged him away. How did you —"

"There'll be time for that later," Taacqan said. "For now, we have to hurry. This is a treasonous business we're on, and if we're caught . . ." he trailed off suggestively.

The other nodded. "Come, then," he said to Kia. "We must meet —"

He was cut short by a scream, tearing suddenly from the throat of one of the women in the group behind him. He whirled, a blade flashing free from his heavy belt; Kia's bo staff snapped into a ready stance; Ryushi's hand was on his sword. For a heart-stopping second, none of them could see the danger; and that sensation was perhaps worse than when their eyes finally fell on what the woman was looking at.

Rising out of the beach, sloughing black sand in a cascade from its narrow shoulders and thin back, was a Jachyra. It was a terrifying scarecrow of a figure, its un-naturally long arms and emaciated legs buried under a motley of belts and rags, sections of its body and face meshed with a dull metal so it was impossible to tell how much of it was flesh and how much was not. The feeble glow of the dark sun glimmered on the lenses of its eyes, one of them telescoping and retracting with a high-pitched whirr as it turned its head to focus on each of the traitors on the beach, settling finally on . . .

About the Author

Chris Wooding was born in Leicester, England, in 1977. Besides *Broken Sky,* he is the author of *Kerosene, Crashing,* and *Endgame,* among others. He is a devout believer in bad horror movies, Anime videos, and the power of coffee.